Civil Blood

A Mirror Lake Mystery

by

Elly Kirsten

Copyright 2017 by Linda Triegel

For information, email **Cozy Cat Press**, cozycatpress@aol.com or visit our website at: www.cozycatpress.com

COZY CAT
P R E S S

ISBN: 978-1-946063-43-4

Printed in the United States of America

Cover design by Paula Ellenberger
www.paulaellenberger.com

1 2 3 4 5 6 7 8 9 10

This book is dedicated to
The cast, crew, and management of the fondly
remembered Candlewood Playhouse
For many smiles in a summer's night.
And to my B&B hosts in Ontario for their unfailing
hospitality.

Two households, both alike in dignity,
In fair Verona, where we lay our scene,
From ancient grudge break to new mutiny,
Where civil blood makes civil hands unclean.
—Romeo and Juliet

Chapter 1

A light mist hung over the still surface of Mirror Lake, blurring the line between sky and water. To his left, the Berkshires loomed a darker gray, but to the right only trees were barely visible. He hoped he'd find the place again.

He found the broken-down gate, where he turned into the woods on an old path that may once have led to a front door. There must have been a house there at one time and he wished it was still there. It might be a good place to hide. But he supposed it was too close to the road, despite the crumbling stone wall along the front of the property.

He walked more slowly now, as the path became harder to see beneath the white pines. The maples and oaks along the lake shore had only just sprouted new green leaves and were easier to see through, but the pines made the day even darker. He needed to get what he came for and out of here before dark. Before he was missed.

He'd seen a cop car when he'd passed the bar on the main drag, but it had turned around and gone back the way it had come. Still, he didn't want to be seen, so he'd left the road for the trail that skirted it, behind the screen of trees.

He stopped, hearing a noise. An animal? He wondered what kinds of animals lived in these woods. He hated the woods, and the nearby town was too damn green too. He'd stood it as long as he could, but now he needed to get back to the city, to sidewalks and warm bars and people he could talk to. But only after he'd got what he came for.

He heard another noise—a curse—and almost laughed. Not a bear or even a fox. Not a problem.

He moved behind a tree to wait until the other man had gone on his way, but he picked the wrong way to turn.

"Who the hell are you?" the other man said, when the two almost ran into each other on the path the walker hadn't realized he'd strayed from.

"I could ask you the same thing," he said, checking out the other man as a potential rival. Had he come for the same thing? How did he know about it? On the other hand, the other man didn't look guilty, just pissed off. He was older too, maybe not in such good shape, although it was hard to tell in the near-darkness.

He tested his theory, saying, "Out of the way, old man," and trying to shove past.

The other man put out a foot and tripped him. He landed on his shoulder, which immediately began to hurt. Must have hit a stone or a root or some damn thing.

"This is my place," the older man said, not raising his rough voice. "Get out."

"Okay, okay! Don't get all bent out of shape. I don't want to be here anyway."

He started to get up, then felt the rock he'd hit lying beneath him. He put his hand on it as if to use it to rise, but as he did, he pulled the rock up with him. He lunged at the other man, who ducked, but not fast enough. The glancing blow knocked him against a tree, and he began to yell.

"Help! Anyone! Help me!"

Nobody could find him here, the younger man thought, getting panicky. He raised the rock again and brought it down hard. The other man fell heavily and was silent.

Damn. Now he'd really have to hustle in case someone heard the shouts. He stared down at the other man, wondering if he was just unconscious, and if he was, should he hit him again. Not that it mattered—the fool couldn't identify him; he'd never seen him before.

The man on the ground didn't move. He took a minute to riffle through the dead man's pockets, thinking he might as well get any money he had on him since he might not find his own stash. Instead, he felt something bulky in a paper wrapping in the man's coat pocket and nearly shouted in triumph.

It was what he'd come for. He supposed the old man must have stumbled on his hidey-hole, but it didn't matter now. Time to get the hell out of here.

Chapter 2

The painting of the purchase of Middleford from the Indians was amateurish, the acrylic paint fading, the frame dusty. It was aligned crookedly, as if too much banging of gavels in the meeting room had knocked it perpetually askew. Diana Quick tilted her head to calculate the degree of misalignment and wondered if she should stop by Town Hall tomorrow with the express purpose of straightening it. She decided instead to wait to see how long it would take someone else to notice.

"Moving right along…"

The dry voice of the acting chairman of the Zoning Commission penetrated Diana's reverie. Shifting in her metal chair, she made an effort to refocus her attention on the business at hand, wishing again, uselessly, that the zoning commission had gotten around to her last month; May's agenda was much longer. May in Middleford meant the start of the summer theater festival season and the general reawakening of business in town—and therefore of town business, whether related to the "world renowned" Middleford Theater Festival or not.

"The season" also brought hordes of tourists to decimate the flowers on the Green and crowd the locals out of all the watering holes within a ten-mile radius, but serious complaints were rare now. Even the most civic-minded citizen recognized that a New England village of scarcely thirty thousand souls, with no industry to speak of and a declining farm population, could count itself fortunate to have attracted such a benign source of dependable revenue. Everyone in town benefited from the festival in one way or another; it brought in both business and favorable press. Scarcely anyone even remembered what Middleford had looked like before the advent of the first theatrical production, under a tent in a field at the end of Hickory Lane, twenty-five years before.

This was not to say that none of the year-round residents decamped between April and October for more remote retreats, renting out their homes in the interim, at exorbitant prices, to visiting celebrities. Nor that everyone had forgotten the sleepy, but historically pristine, village Middleford had been during its first two hundred and eighty years of existence. As the festival embarked on its second quarter century, a small but dedicated band of preservationists were still fighting a rearguard action to prevent the encroachment of the festival into those corners of Middleford as yet unaffected by it. Hence the crowded land-use commission agendas.

The leader of this dauntless band was Bradford Gray, former first selectman, former treasurer, former town clerk, and current chairman of the zoning commission. Brad was a petty tyrant, a fact that was clear to everyone but disregarded by those who deliberately did not look. He helped his friends, and anyone else from whom he wanted a favor in return for a variance from an inconvenient regulation, and outflanked his enemies. Brad was, furthermore, charming, good-looking, and a persuasive speaker who had been elected for his silver tongue and reelected for his ability to get things done—the right things for the right people, which everyone else understood to mean Friends of Brad.

But Bradford Gray was, unaccountably, absent from the May meeting of the Middleford zoning commission.

The meeting had begun late, after a telephone call to Brad's residence had reached only an uninformative answering machine, and another to his cell phone revealed that it had been switched off. At eight-twenty, vice-chairman Seth Howell had taken over the meeting and was now making short work of the long agenda, much to everyone's relief. A short government meeting of any kind in Middleford was as rare as an unacrimonious one.

Seth Howell was also the reason that the board's sympathy unexpectedly shone on Diana—and she nearly missed it. Seth suffered neither fools nor bores gladly, an attitude that did not endear him to those who secretly worried that they might be one or the other. However, the other board members were in their heart of hearts delighted when Seth took charge, and no one interfered with his handling of the meeting.

"Next is final approval of the use of Mrs. Quick's property on the Green as a hotel."

Having phrased the matter as a *fait accompli*, he heard no objection to Diana's opening of the inn she had been planning, preparing, dreaming, and begging Brad Gray and his minions for, for two years. Moving right along, Seth looked at her over the top of his half-glasses and asked, "Is this all your documentation, Mrs. Quick?"

Diana, who had shifted her attention from lopsided artwork to the neat crease in Mark Edwards's slacks and was just at that moment wondering what the artistic director of the festival was doing at this meeting anyway, was startled to find the spotlight on her. Pressed for a hasty answer, she stammered, "Oh—yes. That is, I believe so."

Seth smiled. "I'm sure you're right."

"Mr. Chairman ..."

Ben McIlvey, Bradford Gray's business partner, belatedly stood to speak on his absent colleague's behalf—in opposition, of course, but everyone knew that his objections rose more out of habit than conviction.

"One moment," Seth said mildly, shuffling papers. "We don't appear to have the signed copies from the ladies and gentlemen on the wetlands board. Doris?"

Town clerk Doris Mallory popped up from the front row and disappeared into her office, to emerge a moment later with another set of documents. Ben stood awkwardly for a moment as the members of the board murmured among themselves, then sat down again in as dignified a manner as he could muster.

"Thank you, Mrs. Mallory. Now we are complete, I believe. We wouldn't want to give anyone an excuse to question the board's decisions tonight, would we?"

Seth turned his gaze to Ben once more. It was a look calculated to dry up any pompous rhetoric that might still be brewing in the speaker's throat. They had all heard the arguments before. The other two board members looked at the ceiling, and the townsfolk seated in those irritating metal chairs that seemed designed to force an early adjournment, stifled yawns behind their copies of the agenda. Only Ben was unaware that he had lost his audience and leaped to his feet again at a get-on-with-it wave from Seth.

"Mr. Chairman," he intoned, oblivious to Seth's unsubtle hints that he was wasting his breath and the board's time. "We are concerned that a precedent will be set by granting Mrs. Quick's proposal to run a business in a residential zone. We are particularly concerned that such a business will attract large numbers of transients—"

I certainly hope so, Diana thought, then caught Seth looking at her again, as if he'd read her mind. A faint, conspiratorial smile lit his gray eyes.

"—who will also disrupt the peaceful serenity for which our historic town center is justly famed," Ben finished, at least temporarily. Seth interrupted while Ben was drawing breath.

"Mr. McIlvey, if I may take your points in order," he began in his soft but implacable voice, "Mrs. Quick's great-grandfather's inn was a feature of our historic town center when your raised ranch was not yet a sapling. I must also remind you that the permit to reopen the inn for its original purpose was granted some months ago, based on grandfather rights that seem particularly applicable to this case. And, I may add, despite the objections of certain parties whose ancestors did not have the foresight to buy commercial real estate at 1742 prices. That permit is not in question tonight."

Ben opened his mouth to rebut, but Seth was on a roll. "What we are considering is solely the matter of Mrs. Quick's request to replace her septic tank in order to expand the bathroom facilities that these large numbers of transients, as you call them, will doubtless require after their long journey here from the Big Apple and other points fortunately just as distant. I remind you also, Mr. McIlvey, that this application has been approved by the other land use boards, and your stand here tonight therefore bears an uncanny resemblance to Custer's."

Diana tried not to smile. Any minute now, Seth would bring out his "I'm just a simple country lawyer" speech and floor Ben McIlvey with it. Seth should have been on the festival stage; as it was, he was considered a kind of fringe theater to anyone in town who appreciated a sharp mind and a razor wit. A good many people didn't, of course, which was why he was only vice-chairman of the commission, a fact that Ben McIlvey had temporarily overlooked or, considering that he was really only Bradford Gray's gofer, had disregarded for purposes of his own.

"Mr. Chairman—" Ben began again, ill-advisedly.

Sure enough, Seth snapped at the bait. "I remind you, Mr. McIlvey, that I am in charge of this meeting solely because our illustrious chairman has mysteriously failed to take his rightful place this evening and left us to wait for twenty minutes in vain hope of his resurrection. The rest of us would, therefore, be glad to move the business of the evening along as quickly as possible to make up the time.

"Fortunately," he went on before Ben could dispute this, "we constitute a quorum even without our leader's outsized presence, and as Mrs. Quick's documents are in order, may I have a motion?"

Jesse Connelly took the hint and moved that Diana's application be granted. The motion passed unanimously with no further debate, and Diana was so astonished that she remained seated for several seconds after Ben McIlvey had sat down with a thump and silence had fallen.

"Was there anything else you wanted, Mrs. Quick?" Seth asked.

"No—I mean, is that it?"

"You can pay your fee at the treasurer's office in the morning."

"Oh. Yes, of course." She got up and, avoiding Ben McIlvey's outstretched legs, made her way to the door. "Thank you."

"Our pleasure," Seth said. "Next order of business?"

Chapter 3

Outside Town Hall, Diana drew in a deep breath of night air. It was warm for May; mists lay in the valleys to the west, and a full moon hung over the distant glimmer of Mirror Lake. She could read her watch by its light.

Quarter past nine; she'd been in the meeting scarcely an hour. She heard the door open again behind her, and Beth Hudson, the editor of the *Middleford Weekly Citizen*, emerged.

"Diana, wait a minute, please."

Diana had not actually moved. Her delight over her victory had finally overcome her incredulity, and she had been suppressing the urge to go back inside and kiss Seth Howell. Instead, she smiled at Beth, who was fishing in her capacious shoulder bag for a sharpened pencil. Beth was bright, intuitive, and a good reporter, but she was utterly disorganized in her work habits and dress. Tonight she was wearing a shapeless, although elegantly woven, sleeveless dress over a purple T-shirt. Diana offered her a ballpoint pen.

"Thanks. Well, um—does this mean you'll be able to open the inn for business this summer, Diana?"

"I hope so—at least by August."

"And what will you be calling it?"

"The Inn on the Green." Diana smiled. She might as well call it A Dream Come True.

"What about the actors who are staying there now? Will they have to move?"

Diana had been given zoning-board permission the year before—by a four-to-one vote—to house some of the young apprentices and performers from the Music Faire, the festival theater that offered musicals and comedy, as opposed to the Main Stage, which was the home of Shakespeare and other drama. They received room and board in return for help with the restoration and other chores and were thus not considered paying guests.

"Fortunately not," Diana said. "I have fewer of them with me this summer—twelve, I think—and they will be able to move into the gatehouse when the main building is ready for guests."

"That's the smaller building on the other side of the property? I think you said it used to be the main entrance to the house."

"That's right. I'll be renovating that as well, although not this year. It's solid enough for summer occupancy, however."

"Will you have to go through the permit process again when you start work on that?" Beth asked, obviously recalling Diana's long-running battle with Brad over the inn.

"No, thank goodness."

Beth smiled. "Can I quote you on that?"

"Certainly not!" Fortunately, Beth was discreet as well as clever and managed—how, Diana never understood—to keep her reporting of Bradford Gray's activities factual yet strictly neutral in tone.

"Well, thanks," she said now. "I'd better get back inside before Seth runs through the whole agenda."

"That reminds me," Diana said. "What was Mark Edwards doing in there?"

"Oh, he comes in every spring to get the directional signs for the festival reapproved. It was a condition of the original permit, when your Daniel was First

Selectman. I asked him about it once—Mark Edwards, I mean—why he bothers to attend the meeting in person, and he said he enjoys his once-a-year taste of local government. You notice he was smiling tonight, though. He probably doesn't enjoy us enough to sit in Town Hall for four hours, even if it is only once a year. Oh, one more thing—may I stop by tomorrow to see how the work at the inn is progressing?"

"Make it after five," Diana said. "The actors will be off to rehearsal by then."

"Okay. Thanks, Diana."

"Good night, Beth."

Diana walked around the back of Town Hall and took the path from the lower parking lot that led through a small copse to the old burying ground next to the Congregational church. She normally took this way to Town Hall and back because the path came out on Main Street, near the inn; on a fine night, it was a pleasant stroll.

She walked slowly, enjoying the night and the newly leafed trees she had scarcely noticed earlier in her preoccupation about the outcome of the zoning meeting. Her business had been the sixth item on the agenda, and the board would not normally have got to her before ten. But at eight o'clock, she had been overcome by the conviction that Bradford Gray would move her to the beginning of the meeting in order to engineer a nay vote in her absence—just the kind of move he was famous for—so she had hurried to Town Hall to arrive just as the delayed first business was getting under way. Now it seemed that she had been needlessly anxious.

Brad had consistently opposed Diana's plans to turn her home, which had begun life two hundred years before as a coaching inn, back into a hotel. The argument that Middleford sorely needed more first-class hotels to accommodate the ever-increasing crowds of summer visitors had failed to move him. His own forebears had settled in Middleford before the Civil War, and he was quick to raise their ghosts to protest desecration of their heritage. In Diana's case, this argument was less than effective, since her family, as well as her late husband Daniel's, had been among the original settlers of the town in the 1700's. It was not until generations after the Sedleys and Quicks arrived that Bradford's ancestors had strayed off the Mohawk Trail and stumbled onto the fledgling settlement.

Diana had never quite understood Brad's opposition to the project. It was no skin off his nose if one of the historic homes on the Green became a historic bed-and-breakfast. But Brad hid a mean spirit behind his outward good-fellowship, and Diana had always surmised that he was simply jealous—of Diana's home, her family's longer association with Middleford, and the fact that Daniel Quick had founded the theater festival.

Daniel had never opposed Bradford openly; he had listened to every argument Brad had raised against the best thing to come to town since the stagecoach. Then he had simply gone ahead as if Brad had never opened his mouth. Diana had felt some sympathy for Brad at the time—she had loved Daniel but was well aware of the force of his personality—but of late Brad had become simply a thorn in her side.

Since Daniel's death, Brad had glossed over his lack of foresight about the festival by becoming its leading patron and sponsor—except when it came to the practicalities of housing and feeding visitors. Tourists, in Bradford Gray's opinion, were even lower on the evolutionary ladder than the newest residents of Middleford, escapees from the big city who lived in the subdivisions at the edge of town developed by Brad's architectural firm. That these newcomers had made him nouveau riche as well as old money did not sway him from his opinions.

It was darker in the graveyard now, where the path widened to a gently rising dirt lane winding gracefully through the neatly trimmed plots. Thick, ancient firs and a high iron fence guarded Middleford's Colonial dead. Except for members of families whose plots went back to the founding fathers, no one had been interred in the old burying ground for a hundred years, but Diana felt she knew some of its occupants as well as her living but distant relations.

She stopped by her great-great-grandfather Josiah Sedley's grave near the gate and told him the good news—that the inn he had been forced to close when Middleford had ceased to be a crossroads in the late 1800's would come alive again. Her grandfather, Matthew Sedley, and his parents, Joshua and Hester, rested in the same plot, and she told him too, sure he would share her delight.

She hadn't known Josiah, of course, and Joshua had died young—for a Sedley—but she remembered Hester as a fragile-looking, hummingbird-like creature in her old age. Matthew had preached well into his eighties as minister of the Congregational church on the Green, just down the street from her home, which had been the parsonage at that time.

Matthew had died when Diana was eight, and it was then that the old graveyard had become a refuge for her, a lonely little girl with a vivid imagination, who played on the cool grass and made friends with the names on the tombstones, tracing with a chubby finger their dates and histories and imagining their lives.

She had been the only child, born late in their marriage to an artist father who was too involved in his own world to share much of it with her. Her mother was a social butterfly who was rarely home, and then only to pose with her daughter for the effect of their combined beauty on impressed onlookers.

Diana had tired of the game with the graveyard names finally, when none of the names talked back to her and asked her about her own life. That cool indifference was too much like the living world.

Now the graveyard was simply a shortcut to the library and the new Town Hall, which had replaced the tiny meeting house on the Green. The *Weekly Citizen* occupied that building now. The new Town Hall had been one of Brad Gray's pet projects, and he had boasted about its architectural fidelity to the Colonial spirit, as if to prove he could appreciate something other than converted barns and contemporary chalets.

Seth's remark about those original settlers who had not had the foresight to see which pieces of Middleford real estate would appreciate in value over two centuries came back to Diana and confirmed her suspicions about Bradford Gray's jealousy of her and all her kind. She thought she would make a point to be pleasant to him the next time they met, to show she harbored no ill feelings. On the other hand, he might see that as condescension. One never knew with Brad.

It was getting cool again, and Diana was wearing only a denim jacket over her slacks and cotton sweater. She quickened her steps, passing the small, sad group of Civil War graves without a second glance. Middleford's only genuine hero—and the one member of his family Bradford Gray could legitimately boast about—was buried there. Captain Gurden Gray had fallen at Gettysburg after being promoted from the ranks for his bravery at Fredericksburg and Chancellorsville; his tomb was appropriately large and, since Brad had nothing to do with the design, pleasingly simple, with only the captain's name and dates carved into the unusually well-maintained white Vermont marble.

The path turned there, to give The Hero a respectful space, and led into the trees that shadowed the stone wall along the Green. Looking up, searching for the moon behind the clouds, Diana tripped, caught herself, then tripped again over some object too large to step over easily.

She fell, unhurt, onto something soft but unyielding. Putting her hand out to help herself back up, she touched the something. It blocked the entire path.

Then the moon reemerged and revealed a male figure lying across the path, its head partially obscured by the soft earth and moss at the edge of the trees. The part that was visible shone dully in the moonlight, and the dark, matted hair mingled with a substance that gleamed like. . .

Diana sat back on the gravel path and clamped both hands to her mouth to stifle a scream.

The chairman of the zoning board had not just missed a meeting.

Bradford Gray was dead.

Chapter 4

Diana wasn't sure how long she had knelt beside Bradford Gray's body. Had she fainted? No, she never did that. But she did not remember moving to the stone bench near the outer wall of the burying ground, about twenty feet away, although when feeling finally returned and her brain began to function, she realized it must have been several minutes. All she remembered thinking as she knelt, stunned, on the grassy verge was, *It's only flesh and blood ... it's not really Brad....*

She must be in shock. She sat on the bench for perhaps ten minutes more, not looking up from her hands folded in her lap, thinking, remembering, deliberately recalling only long-past events so she would not think about how she had found Brad.

The last death she'd seen had been her husband Daniel's, dying in her arms after his second heart attack. She had been able to comfort him, assure him that she would be fine, that she would always love him. In the end, his death had not been as hard as she had expected—not nearly so hard as the fearful anticipation, in the year after his first, milder heart attack, that it could happen again at any time.

It was not death that frightened her, she had discovered, nor blood, nor even violence; it was the anticipation, and then the memory afterward of pain and illness. Her cursedly vivid imagination insisted on reliving events in a dozen different versions.

She would not sleep well tonight.

"Diana? Diana, are you all right?"

Her eyes focused on Nigel Henson's slim, graceful figure, from his neat brown hair to his denim jacket down to his LL Bean mocs, spotless even in the mud. One of the actors who currently lived at the inn, Nigel was the only one who had been with the festival before, the only one she considered a friend.

She remembered now. He had promised to walk over to Town Hall and meet her at about ten; she had estimated that her part of the meeting would be over by then.

"What time is it?" she said, grasping at the mundane to reconnect to reality.

"Not quite ten."

"Was it you who called 911?"

"Yes. Fortunately, I had my cell phone with me; I wouldn't have wanted to leave you alone. The ambulance and police came a few minutes ago."

"That's all right ... I'd have been all right," Diana reassured him. She must have told him to call the police, but she couldn't remember. She supposed it would all come back to her later.

She became aware of blacker shadows in the gray darkness, blocking her view of the path between her and Brad's body. Someone was running a yellow plastic tape around the wall, getting it snared in fir branches; someone else was setting up a camera on a tripod near the ...

She stared at the group of men, envisioning the body as she had first seen it, or half seen it, trying to keep her imagination under control. Suddenly a bank of floodlights blazed to life inside the graveyard, invading the domain of the dead.

Diana closed her eyes. Nigel, more used to spotlights, focused on the men on the path, but then returned his attention to Diana, who was staring straight ahead, clutching her arms and shivering. He took off his jacket and draped it over her shoulders. After a moment she looked up again.

"Thank you."

"Don't you want to go home?"

"I can't yet," she said tiredly. "Kent wants to talk to me." She remembered that now. Police Chief Kent Brewster had helped her to the bench, sat her down, and told her to stay put. It was all coming back. The reality would surely be a relief.

"Oh." Nigel sat down next to her, prepared to wait as long as she did. Diana smiled, grateful for his uncharacteristic silence. He would normally have plied her with questions, but he had apparently seen enough for himself and was willing to wait for details.

Nigel had been the first of her actor guests to take up residence at the inn last winter, and one of the few classically trained actors among the musical performers she usually took in. He was also the only Brit among them, although several visiting stars over the years had been British, Canadian, and even—as Nigel had noted with a beautifully executed sneer—from *Hollywood*. Nigel, apart from being able to choose his roles, his friends, and his time off as he liked, was also the only one who could afford to live where he liked, inherited money freeing him from dependence on an actor's salary.

When he'd first come to the festival three years before, he was alone in a strange country, and he'd quickly recognized Diana as a familiar landmark, someone who knew London as well as he did. Diana told herself she shouldn't show favoritism among her charges, but if she didn't, Nigel would be even more alone. He was a charming escort—and occasional cook, housekeeper, and gardener—when she needed one. And since he was a dozen years younger than she was, she told herself he was safe from gossip. She treated him like the friend she needed. She wasn't quite sure how he saw her.

And Nigel knew when to be discreet. Now he watched the movement around Captain Gray's tomb wordlessly, seemingly oblivious to Diana. But when two hefty deputies suddenly straightened up, raising something between them, he turned to her and said, "What happened at the meeting?"

"What?" For an instant, she couldn't think what he was talking about, but then she remembered and couldn't help smiling. "I got it," she said. "I can open the inn this summer, if I like."

He grinned. "That's fantastic! Congratulations." He leaned over to give her a hug, and it was only when he let her go that she realized he'd deftly shielded her from the sight of Bradford Gray's body being carried out the gate on a stretcher. He didn't know her inner self well enough to know that she would have preferred to see, preferred her experienced eyes to take it all in so that her still-childlike imagination would not see greater horror.

"Does this mean they're finally going to fill that enormous hole in your yard?" he asked.

She refocused on what he was saying, bringing her mind back to the mundane. "When they bring in the new septic tank, yes. I'm afraid it's going to be a mess for several more weeks, though."

"Looks like the second act set of bloody *Les Miserables*," Nigel grumbled. "But at least the end is in sight."

The floodlights suddenly went off, leaving only an anemic Coleman lantern to guide Deputy Charlie Pettibone, who was revealed as the officer carefully draping police-scene tapes over the tombstones surrounding the trampled ground where Brad had lain. Police Chief Brewster stood under a tree talking in a low voice to a man in a trenchcoat carrying a black bag—Dr. Sunderland, Diana realized. A retired surgeon, he must be the part-time medical examiner now, the person the town called on when they couldn't get the regular coroner out from the state barracks fast enough.

After saying good night to Dr. Sunderland, Chief Brewster shuffled toward them. His craggy face was drawn in the dim light, and the usual circles under his eyes looked darker than ever. Diana felt more pity for him than she had for Brad.

"I'm sorry, Kent," she said gently. "I know you were his best friend."

Kent Brewster tipped his hat over the back of his head and sat down on a flat-topped headstone facing her. "I guess I was his only friend—or at least the only one who still talked to him. Lately ... well, I wish we'd talked more." His attention drifted away for a moment, and he added only, "We started grade school together, in kindergarten, you know. So long ago ..."

"What precisely happened here, Chief?" Nigel asked in a tone Diana recognized from a J.B. Priestley mystery drama he'd been in last season. Diana introduced him to Kent, who eyed him assessingly and then resumed his professional manner.

"It looks like he slipped on the mud to the side of the path and fell back on that little step in front of that low tombstone," he said, pointing. "There's some blood on the stone and a hell of a hole in the back of Brad's head—sorry, Diana. Don't mean to remind you ... I mean ..."

He took a deep breath. "I can't figure what he was doing here, though."

"He must have been on his way to the zoning meeting," Diana said. "He was late. He may have had car trouble and then taken a shortcut through the burying ground, the way I did."

Kent looked at her, his gaze sharper. "You came this way going *to* the meeting? What time was that?"

"About five past eight, I think. I was a little late myself, but my business was later in the agenda." Diana remembered her distrust of Brad, her suspicions about his motives, but she didn't regret them. His behavior had been what it had been, and just because Brad was dead was no reason to pretend he was a wonderful human being. Anyway, it was easier to think of him as he had been—obstructive, stubborn, self-aggrandizing. But alive.

"You didn't see Brad on your way to Town Hall?" Kent asked, dragging her back to the present.

"No. It wasn't quite dark yet. I think I'd have noticed if anyone else had been here."

"You didn't see anyone at all?"

"No."

"What about you?" Kent turned suddenly to Nigel, who, the last word in unflappable, didn't even blink.

"I came to escort Mrs. Quick home from the meeting. It was over earlier than she'd anticipated, so I only came as far as this place before I met her—or rather, found her. She was somewhat distressed, as you may imagine."

"What time did you leave the meeting?" Kent asked, addressing Diana again.

"About quarter past nine. I told you before, remember?" She did remember everything now; she had talked to Kent briefly before Nigel dragged her away and made her sit down and close her eyes. She had felt faint, she recalled. "The meeting finished early," she said, "or at least, my part of it did."

"Oh, sure. Sorry," he apologized again. Kent's gaze wandered to the wall, the path, then back to the cordoned-off area where Charlie Pettibone stood at conscientious attention.

Nigel spoke up. "May I see Mrs. Quick home now, Chief? She's had an upsetting night, and it's getting rather chilly here."

Kent glanced at Nigel as if he'd forgotten he was there, but after a moment his eyes focused again. "Sure. Didn't mean to keep you. I'll see you again tomorrow, Diana, okay?"

"Of course." Diana and Nigel stood up. Kent remained slumped on the headstone, his folded hands drooping between his knees. Diana bent down and kissed his cheek. "Good night, Kent."

He didn't respond.

Chapter 5

Diana and Nigel walked in silence up Main Street. The town Green, stretching three blocks beyond the burying ground, looked gray in the midnight damp, and the widely spaced street lamps cast a diminished glow through the haze. They passed no one else, and no cars entered the twenty-mile-an-hour road that ringed the Green. The residents in this part of town went to bed early.

Nigel maintained his comforting silence, but Diana found her mind wandering back into speculation she would rather have avoided. When had Brad entered the burying ground? If he had indeed come that way, it must have been because he was delayed somewhere on his route to Town Hall. Perhaps someone had buttonholed him to ask a favor or plead a cause.

But that meant he would have been on foot, which didn't make sense either. Brad lived some distance from Town Hall and normally on meeting nights, he pulled his BMW into the parking lot at the dot of eight.

"How was rehearsal today?" she asked Nigel, to fill the stillness and silence the questions in her mind. She didn't know if Nigel would understand that she preferred noise to evocative silence and didn't much care what he said, although he always had amusing things to say about his work.

He was appearing as Mercutio in *Romeo and Juliet,* and as she expected, he launched into a vivid description of his day, including scurrilous remarks about his director and fellow actors. He was getting into his Queen Mab speech, transforming the Green into the alleys of Verona, as they neared the inn.

"And in this state she gallops night by night
Through lovers' brains, and then they dream of love
..."

"Hullo, what's all that?" he said suddenly, falling out of character.

Closer to Diana's house, even Nigel's recitation and the thick night air couldn't mask the noise coming from inside, as if a party were going on. The big white house stood well back from the Green, with a circular driveway, a holdover from its coaching inn days when this was the yard of the inn and the entrance to the stables where the coaches came after depositing their passengers at the front door.

They passed through the small door set in the stone wall to the right of the two large wrought-iron gates, now closed, and into the parking area, presently containing only Diana's Volvo, Nigel's Miata, an ancient VW mini-bus shared by several of the actors, and the town car with the inn's logo already, expectantly, stenciled on it. Diana had easily won concession from the zoning commission to put another parking lot in the town center by setting aside a full acre, spread inconspicuously around the spacious, tree-studded grounds of the old inn, for guests' cars.

"Bloody cheek," Nigel said indignantly. "It's quiet hours."

In an attempt to rein in youthful enthusiasm and prevent the neighbors from complaining to the police, Diana had set designated hours—usually just before or after rehearsals and performances—when noise and high spirits would be tolerated in the house. Anyone violating quiet hours during the rest of the day or night would be sent back to the community college dorm, a dire if empty threat that had thus far been wonderfully effective. Tonight, however—and it was after eleven by now—everyone in the house seemed to be violating the rule at the same time.

"It's a revolution," Nigel said accusingly.

Diana smiled, for she had made out the unmistakable strains of "For he's a jolly good fellow," drifting out the ground-floor windows. Occasional howls from Molly, the Irish Setter that belonged to one of the actors, accompanied the chorus.

"No," she said, "it's a celebration. Come on, let's find out what the occasion is."

The celebrants had been thoughtful enough to close the windows and not extend the party to the verandah, but every light in the house seemed to be on, and when Nigel opened the door for her, Diana saw that the rug in the living room—soon to become the inn's reception area—had been rolled back.

Someone's CD player was on, but the London cast recording of *Jesus Christ Superstar* seemed to be playing to deaf ears. Bodies in constant motion drifted in and out of the kitchen, danced to tunes out of their own heads on the bare floor, or stood around the grand piano, where they took turns making more noise.

Attempting to count heads, Diana decided that more than her allotted boarders had infiltrated the house, and a moment later a gang of them lifted Steve Bannerman bodily and began carrying him around the parlor on the shoulders of two chorus boys from the Music Faire. Most of her guests worked there, and a friendly rivalry had always existed between the musical performers and the classically trained actors, like Nigel, who played Shakespeare and Chekhov at the Main Stage instead of Stephen Sondheim and Andrew Lloyd Webber at the Music Faire.

Diana began to feel more purposeful as she glanced around, wondering if anyone had thought to provide food or drink, or had brought in extra chairs—not that anyone was sitting down. She had long since removed the antiques and breakables to her private part of the house.

Michelle Matson, a pretty redheaded dancer who was Steve's love interest this season, spotted Diana and rushed up to her, gushing.

"He got the part!" she shrieked. "Steve got the title role—the lead—in *Jesus Christ Superstar!* Rehearsals start Friday! Annie is Mary. I'm one of the Apostles' women. Isn't it too terrific?"

"Oh, gawd," Nigel groaned in mock horror. "I suppose we're going to have to call him 'sir' now."

Michelle tugged Nigel's hair and squealed with delight before running off to maul someone else. The noise hardly abated as Diana's presence became generally known, and no one even stood still. But they didn't simply mill around aimlessly the way most people did at a party; their movements were almost choreographed. Steve, a big, good-looking blond who was immensely popular with everyone, was grinning idiotically. When he gained the floor again, the crowd moved around him as if he were a maypole. Snatches of songs and dance steps they remembered from last season or were rehearsing for this one broke out in graceful sequence.

Diana couldn't help smiling at their infectious joy. Steve deserved the tribute, as the first member of the chorus in years to rise from the ranks and be given a leading part, but it took less reason than that to have a party.

Nigel looked as if he wanted to join in, but instead asked Diana if she wanted him to call a halt. "After all, they don't know about—"

Diana put a hand on his arm to stop him. "Don't tell them. Let it wind down, and then tell them about the zoning permit. Forget about the other thing until tomorrow. I don't want to spoil the fun."

And, she thought, she didn't want to have to tell the story yet again. Time enough for that tomorrow. Perhaps Nigel would tell them for her, and she could safely think of something else.

Absorbing the merriment, she began to feel her energy coming back and her hostessing instincts reawakening. It wasn't all that late, by inn and theater standards, and she had guests to look after—even if they were non-paying practice guests.

"In fact," she added, already feeling the guilt of her cowardly evasion, "why don't you send someone down to the Cyn Bin for a case of beer. Cynthia is usually there until midnight, even if she closes early. My treat."

Nigel grinned. "You *are* a glutton for punishment— but thanks."

He sent one of the chorus boys off to the theater crowd's favorite watering hole, run by Cynthia Howell and popularly referred to as the Cyn Bin, and Diana forged her way into the melee to congratulate Steve, who caught her up in a bear hug and blurted out, "I'm so *verklempt!*"

"He's been waiting years to say that," said Anne Richmond, the tall, slim brunette who, according to Michelle, had been cast as Mary Magdalene to Steve's Jesus in the second musical production of the season, opening in July. Steve ignored her.

"Hey, Mistress Quickly, now that I'm a star, do I get a special rate for gracing this fine establishment with my presence?"

"I should make you *pay* now," Diana countered when she got her breath back. "People who get top billing can't expect free lodging too."

"Oh, it's Judas who gets top billing," someone else told her. "And *he's* renting a house of his own."

"There's a lesson there," Jim Bishop began portentously, only to be threatened with a barrage of donuts—apparently the only party food around. Jim, a singer with ill-concealed ambitions to join the acting company, walked a fine line between tolerance and ostracism. He backed off with, "But I'm blowed if I know what it is!"

A donut flung at Jim missed him and sprinkled powdered sugar on Diana before landing in the rubber plant beside the front door. Michelle doubled up with giggles, but Jim, who would normally have quelled her with a look, paid no attention. He was staring at the door, open-mouthed, and Diana turned around to see what he was looking at.

There, filling her doorway, was this season's Middleford Festival celebrity guest star, Alex Gordon.

He'd apparently knocked and not been heard, so came in barely in time to sidestep the flying donut. Now he was gazing at the crowd with a faint smile on his mouth and a twinkle in his light blue eyes. Diana couldn't help staring too; she'd never met anyone whose eyes really did twinkle, but on Alex Gordon it wasn't just a figure of speech.

He stood there, tall and cool in a casual but exquisite combination of light wool slacks and Armani jacket, perfectly still in a relaxed way, as if he knew he'd be noticed eventually. His graying dark hair was neatly groomed and his strong chin looked freshly shaved. He stood with casual ease, as if he had the run of the house and knew it. *Star quality*, Diana thought wonderingly; *it still existed.*

Someone else saw him, and then someone else, and gradually a hush fell over the room as his presence pushed everything else out of it, like a vacuum drawing out air. Even Molly lay down, put her head on her paws, and looked up adoringly.

"Now, then," he said, in a low, slightly husky voice that still carried, just as it did on a stage. "What's all this about?"

Chapter 6

"Criminy!" Nigel murmured into the vacuum. "It's D.C. Dickson."

There were a few titters, and the atmosphere relaxed slightly, but still no one else spoke. Nigel was only acknowledging what everyone recognized—a characteristic tag line from the British television crime series that had made Alex Gordon famous twenty years before. That persona had clung to him, but the awestruck silence also recognized the work that had afterwards set Alexander Gordon on the circuitous theatrical path to guest-starring roles in American Shakespearean productions.

He gave no indication of having heard Nigel's remark, however, and his blue eyes found Diana. He smiled, and she was disconcerted to find her knees going weak, as if she were a teenager being introduced to her first celebrity—which was absurd, since she had met scores of them. Alex Gordon was no different. She wondered if he remembered that they had met before, but it seemed unlikely. It was the year she married Daniel, and she had been very much in his shadow, with very little presence of her own.

"Mrs. Quick?" he asked, holding out his hand and pretending not to notice her bemusement.

She supposed he was used to speechless admirers, but she found herself annoyed at her own lack of aplomb. She should have learned better in the fifteen years since they first met. Still, her hostess's training belatedly overcame her reactions and she asked, "How may I help you, Mr. Gordon?"

"Mrs. Peterson at the accommodation bureau gave me your name. She thought you might be able to put me up for a few days. My business in New York finished early, so I decided to come directly here. Unfortunately, I seemed to have caused no end of nuisance by doing so, including arriving on your doorstep at this late hour. I tried to call, but there was no answer—"

A strangled sound at the back of the room told Diana that at least one of her boarders had heard the telephone earlier and ignored it and was now kicking himself. She couldn't help smiling, and regathering some of her lost aplomb, as she motioned for Alex Gordon to follow her out of the room.

"Nigel," she said on the way out, "can you keep this mob under control for a little longer?"

"No problem," he said agreeably. "I expect they're ready to break up anyway. They'd rather gossip under the bedcovers now, I'm sure."

"Thank you." In the hallway, Diana closed the connecting door to the living room behind her and addressed her visitor, who waited politely for her to respond to his request.

"I wish I could help, Mr. Gordon," she said, "but I'm afraid the house is in the midst of renovations, and all the finished rooms are occupied. Did you try the motels outside town? Perhaps one of the private homes that take guests?"

"The ever-obliging Mrs. Peterson made numerous telephone calls on my behalf, but apparently all the alternative lodgings are overflowing as the result of an inconveniently timed realtors' convention."

She wondered at the back of her mind why he didn't pull rank and insist on first-class accommodations, but did not ask. She knew he had a reputation for being easy to get along with, and she had found from her own experience that the more successful an actor was, the less he felt he had to throw his weight around. Still, there were plenty of egotistical exceptions, and she wasn't prepared to fall under Alex Gordon's spell within five minutes of his crossing her threshold.

"I *have* rented a house for the season, but the owners won't be out of it for another fortnight," he explained, and ventured, "Mrs. Peterson said something about a gatehouse?"

"Oh. Well, yes, I suppose you could stay there, but it isn't very comfortable. And it's been shut up all winter, so it may be mildewy ..."

"I assure you, I've endured worse."

"Very well—if you're sure." *Good heavens*, she thought frantically, *was the bed clean? Were there enough sheets and blankets and towels in the cupboard? Should she ask him to pay? Would he expect breakfast? Why couldn't people wait until she was ready to open for business! Drat Enid Peterson.*

But she schooled her expression to conceal her doubts and asked him to wait while she collected the appropriate linens. He took them from her, adjusted them under one arm, picked up his solitary overnight bag with the other hand, and said, "Lead the way."

She found herself explaining as they picked their way over the obstacle course that the septic installers had made of the lawn, "It's not really a gatehouse anymore, since the new driveway was put in. The old pike road ran along what is now the back of the house, and the gate was there in the mid-eighteen hundreds. Nowadays, there's no access to the road, so at least you will have privacy."

He looked around him with interest at the parts of the house that were lit by outdoor floodlights and the bits of yard that weren't covered by incipient septic installation. "How old is the house?"

"Parts of it go back to 1764, twenty-two years after the town was founded. My father always claimed we staked the first homestead in Middleford, but there's no proof of that. Up to about 1860 the house was a coaching inn, but when the railroad came through, my great-great-grandfather closed the inn. He was stubborn about the sorts of people who stayed in his house, and he thought anyone who rode the railway was automatically a lower class of person."

"I'm grateful he's not around to see who's about to occupy his gatehouse. My blood is far from blue; I was born in Nova Scotia and raised in Birmingham, and I rode the tube to work for years before I made enough money to afford taxis."

Diana smiled in the darkness. "Oh, I don't think Josiah was too fussy about what sort of person hung about the *outbuildings.*"

He laughed and then asked some interested questions about her ancestors while she unlocked the gatehouse and flicked the light switch. Fortunately, the lights worked, and the old place didn't look as bad as she had feared. It was a miniature version of the main house, with a large sitting room, master bedroom, and kitchen downstairs, with several under-the-eaves bedrooms and baths above.

"Doesn't smell musty to me," he remarked.

"You needn't be polite," she said, but silently gave thanks to her housekeeper, who must have remembered to keep the cottage vacuumed and dusted. "I'll give it a good airing tomorrow," she said, "if you haven't decided to clear out by then."

"I doubt that," he said, in a tone that told her nothing but rang in her mind oddly, as if it contained undertones she could not comprehend.

She moved to take the bed linens from him, but he stopped her. "I can make my own bed," he said, putting them down on the seat of an armchair.

"As you like." She showed him the sitting room—the fireplace was clean, she noted with relief—and added as she checked the cupboards in the kitchen, "I'm afraid the stove doesn't work. You can have a microwave tomorrow, but if you're hungry, come back to the house tonight and we'll find you something to eat."

He smiled. "I'm not sure I want to face that mob again."

The sounds of merriment, only slightly subdued despite Nigel's prediction, still came from the house. "I'll bring something over, then."

"Nonsense. I can manage until tomorrow."

"As you like," she repeated. "When would you want breakfast?"

"You needn't trouble," he said. "There must be a diner in town—or even a McDonald's."

"Heaven forbid." She began a laugh, but then choked it back, remembering that it had been Bradford Gray who led the charge against allowing any sort of fast-food establishment within five miles of the historic town center. That had been one of his few crusades that enlisted the support of the majority of Middleford's citizens, and the result of the campaign was a limited number of eating establishments in the center of town but a refreshing lack of arches and boiling-oil aromas.

"What?" he said, apparently intrigued by the changing expression on her face.

She shook her head. "Sorry. It's a long story. But this is an inn, however ramshackle it may look at the moment, and there is plenty of food in the larder. Just come over to the kitchen whenever you care to in the morning."

"Thank you."

She said good night, then, eager to leave so he could settle in—and to give herself a little distance from him. She needed to think about this unexpected intrusion into her life. He might well be less trouble than sewer excavation, contentious town government regulations, and unburied bodies, but an instinct she hadn't felt for a long time told her that Alex Gordon could easily become a large part of her life—if she let him. The pleasure of an adult conversation was too tempting, the enjoyment of watching his handsome, mobile face react to what she had to say with understanding too enticing.

But he had let her go—more, she thought, because he sensed her withdrawal than because he just wanted to get to bed—and she walked slowly back to the house, lost in thought.

Chapter 7

Even after the celebration in the parlor had ended and the house was her own again, Diana found she could not sleep. But it was not Alex Gordon that kept her awake. She undressed for bed and lay down on it, but then found her mind, released from the distraction of light and noise, retracing her steps to Town Hall, back through the burying ground, then to the discovery of Bradford Gray's body lying on the grass, as lifeless as the marble surrounding him. She told herself she should not dwell on that, should think instead of the party in Steve's honor, the unexpected eruption into her life of the extremely attractive Alex Gordon.

No, she did not want to think about him either, especially in the light of an attractive male. He had been attractive fifteen years ago, too, but in a rough-cut way; he hadn't had the polish he'd acquired since. He certainly hadn't held a candle to Daniel, who was in his prime then, vital yet mature, devilishly handsome yet distinguished looking. Diana had never questioned what Daniel saw in her, but considered herself fortunate to have caught his interest. She'd never regretted marrying him, nor been disillusioned by him in any way.

She rose finally, saw that it was half-past four—she must have drifted off at least briefly—and dressed. She might as well start cleaning up downstairs, if she was going to remain wakeful. The living room must be a shambles. She put on an old pair of jeans and a sweatshirt emblazoned with last year's festival logo, and went downstairs.

Much to her surprise, the parlor was nearly spotless. She contemplated it, wondering whom she—or at any rate, her housekeeper—had to thank for it. Nigel, perhaps, though he'd never admit it. She decided to leave well enough alone and not look for any stray glasses or donut holes. Instead, she went into the kitchen to set up breakfast makings for the morning. She habitually left clean dishes, breakfast cereal in glass containers, and utensils on the counter, as well as juice and other perishables in the extra-large refrigerator, for early risers.

When she had finished checking supplies, she made a cup of tea and took it out onto the verandah, pausing to look up at the hazy, nearly vanished moon. The night was still mild, still a little damp. They might have an early summer after all.

Alex Gordon was sitting on the top step.

"I saw your lights go on," he said, looking up at her.

"Did you change your mind about getting something to eat?"

"No, but I'll have a cup of whatever that is you're drinking—it smells like good old English Breakfast."

Automatically, she said, "Of course. Come in."

She led the way back into the kitchen and motioned him to sit down. He pulled out one of the chairs at the oak table and sat down while she turned the burner on again under the kettle. There was silence until the kettle began to whistle. She took it off the stove, poured water over a freshly filled tea ball, and handed it to him. There was already a spoon and a sugar bowl on the table.

"Milk?"

"Yes, please."

She got it for him and sat down, watching him jiggle the tea ball as the water got darker.

"You still have an English taste in tea," she observed. "Dark and milky."

He smiled. "Some things stay with you. I remember sitting around my mother's kitchen table when I was a kid, listening to my aunts gossip and pinching another slice of cake when they lit into the neighbors' sleeping arrangements and weren't watching me."

"Oh," she said. "I'm sorry. I should have offered you something to go with that."

"Thank you, no. Just the tea is fine."

"I've got a Battenburg cake."

That stopped him. "You don't really!" he said, astonished.

"Honestly. Would you like a slice?"

"I can't resist. It's been donkey's years since I've seen one. Where do you get them?"

"I'm not sure I ought to tell you. You may buy up my sole source of supply."

She got out the iced, pink-and-white cake, cut off several slices, and placed the dish and a fork near him, so he could help himself. He dug in, going through the first rich, almondy slice quickly, but slowing down as he consumed a second.

"I take it you're not English-born either?" he said. "You have a slight accent, but you talked about this being your family home."

He had not remembered her. She should have felt relieved, even flattered, rather than disappointed. "I was born in Middleford," she told him, "but my late husband was posted to London toward the end of his career."

He ate a forkful of cake, apparently giving himself time to digest all that she had revealed about herself in that one sentence.

"Posted?" he said finally.

"He was a diplomat. After he died, I came back here. That was four years ago."

"And you're glad you did?"

She sipped her tea, thinking about that. Glad didn't begin to describe the sense of achievement she'd felt lately, the growing contentment attached to being in her own place and living her life as she never had before, just for her own satisfaction. She'd forgotten all that in the nuisance of permits and contractors and perpetual messiness, but it came back to her now.

"It's been ... satisfying," she said at last, and smiled.

"Tell me."

And, surprising herself, she did. She told him how she had returned home after Daniel's death, not knowing what she would make of the rest of her life, and caring little; how the familiar, once-loved town had, with the help of a few precious friends there who didn't care that she had deserted them for years, gradually enfolded her again; how she had the idea of reopening the old inn and letting life back into it. And into her heart as well, although she didn't admit that detail to him.

He was a good listener, interrupting only to encourage her to go on. When she finally wound down, he asked, "Is everything a go now—for the inn, I mean? Mrs. Peterson said something about your still needing some permit or other."

Diana wondered what else Enid had said; she had a tongue that ran on wheels, and she took her position at the accommodation bureau as license to poke her long nose into everyone else's home life. Enid had been one of those who had viewed Diana as a deserter when she married Daniel and moved abroad. "I suppose she thinks she's too sophisticated for her hometown," was the sentiment that ran like an undercurrent in her later relations with some of her former neighbors. Daniel had, of course, told her to pay no attention, but that was easier said than done.

"No, it's all approved now," was all she told Alex.

Reminded again of Brad, whom she'd almost succeeded in forgetting, she realized that it would be impossible not to think about him often during the next few days. But perhaps, if she told Alex about Brad, too, about who he was to her and the rest of Middleford, she might at least not wake herself up at night with images of Brad's lifeless body taking over her mind. So she told him that story too.

When she had finished, he said only, "It must have been a shock for you." His eyes were sympathetic, but when he reached out a hand, as if to take hers in a comforting gesture, she hid her own in her lap, pretending she hadn't noticed.

"Yes ... although perhaps not in the way you think. We were never friends. Brad had a vast number of acquaintances but very few friends." She thought about Kent Brewster and hoped he was not sleepless tonight too.

Alex looked thoughtfully across the room. She followed his gaze and saw by the wall clock that it was gone six a.m. Good heavens. She hadn't exchanged this kind of pre-dawn confidences with anyone since college, although Daniel had been a morning person, and she had accommodated her schedule to his. She wasn't in the least tired, but she glanced at Alex, wondering if she had kept him up. But he was looking only pensive, not sleepy.

She watched him covertly, noticing the lines around his eyes, the elegant curve of his profile from temple to chin. But then her gaze caught on his hand as he lifted his cup—a large, square, strong hand, like a workman's. Of course, he had been a manual laborer before he took up acting; that was a well-known part of his official biography, but she hadn't realized what an odd contrast it made with his elegant head. The aristocratic ditch-digger.

She looked away, conscious suddenly of her own appearance. She fingered the blunt cut of her auburn hair—Daniel had liked it long, but last year she had cut it into a more practical style—and smoothed her hand over her own cheek and chin. No sagging yet, she thought, unless she was deceiving herself. All at once she wished for a mirror.

"What was he doing in the graveyard?" Alex asked, seemingly out of nowhere. He looked back at her, his gaze penetrating now.

Trusting that her embarrassing lapse into schoolgirl vanity didn't show on her face, she shrugged, then followed his train of thought. Brad, of course. He was talking about Brad.

"No one seems to know," she said. "My guess was that he had car trouble and decided to walk to Town Hall."

"Did he live far away?"

"Yes, in Long Ridge Estates—one of the posher housing developments surrounding the town." She drew a rough map of the town on the tabletop with her finger, keeping her mind firmly on where Brad had lived, not where he had died. She placed the sugar bowl at Town Hall and the creamer at the Green.

"Couldn't he have gotten a ride?"

"Perhaps not, if he'd broken down on the way."

"Did anyone find his car?"

"I don't know ... what are you getting at?" she asked, her attention fully caught now. Where *would* Brad have left his car that would have made a short cut through the burying ground a useful alternative route? She hadn't noticed a car on the Green when she and Nigel walked home, and she would have if it had been there.

In fact, a town ordinance forbade overnight parking along the Green. She frowned.

He looked at her until she met his gaze.

"Is there any chance his death wasn't an accident?"

Chapter 8

Diana stared at him, wondering if he could possibly be serious—as if her own mind hadn't been groping toward the same conclusion. "You're letting D.C. Dickson get the better of you," she said accusingly.

He grinned. "No, but don't think I don't take advantage of him every chance I get. He gets me into the most amazing places."

"But if you're not letting your imagination run wild, what could possibly have given you the idea that Brad didn't die accidentally?"

"I *am* letting my imagination run wild. It's what I do for a living, remember? I'm also paid to be observant."

She dismissed this reasoning with an impatient wave of her hand. "I'm sure it never occurred to the police that it was anything but an accident. Or to me, for that matter, and I was there." *If she'd ever whistled in the wind,* she thought, *this was the time.* He'd only voiced what she had been afraid to suggest.

"So you were." He considered her for a moment and then, as if failing to read any further information in her face, said, "Look—indulge me for a moment. It won't go any further than this kitchen if you say so, and if I'm completely off the mark, at least I'll have learned something about my new hometown. You've told me a little about the man who was—who died. Tell me who his friends and enemies were, who benefits from his death, whom has he ticked off lately?"

Diana grimaced, trying not to smile. He interpreted her look correctly and said, "I see. It's a wide field. Well, was he married?"

"Yes, but I don't think—"

"Happily married?"

"I don't really know what Brad and Marjorie's relationship was. We weren't particularly friendly. Our interests weren't the same." *That was putting it mildly,* she thought. "I'll concede that in public they never seem—seemed—a particularly loving couple. They rarely even appeared at the same functions together, and common gossip has it that they hadn't slept in the same bedroom for years, but they still lived under the same roof. One shouldn't make assumptions from gossip, of course, even if he was a public figure, and one would think she ..."

"Would stand by her man?" He smiled, though with understanding at her reluctance to indulge in "common gossip."

"I don't know Marjorie well," she went on doggedly, "not well enough to guess what she thought about his public life or what she would feel about his—about losing Brad."

She was still having trouble thinking of Bradford Gray in the past tense, which was crazy. They hadn't been any better friends than she and Marjorie. It shouldn't matter to her. And yet ... a memory came to her out of a forgotten past. She as a little girl, walking home alone, happily talking to her imaginary friends, then being set upon by a group of slightly older boys who, hearing her, began to tease, not letting up. Brad, short, stocky, but fearless, saw them and interfered, sending the other boys on their way and seeing Diana the rest of the way home, ignoring her tears, saying nothing until he left her at her door. "They won't bother you again," he told her then. And they hadn't.

She went on, "Marjorie had money when they were married, so she wouldn't benefit financially from Brad's death, although I suppose there was life insurance. And Brad's business was apparently doing well."

"What about his business partners?"

"He had only one—Ben McIlvey. And he was at the zoning meeting."

"What about his business dealings? Were they on the up-and-up?"

"I never heard anything to the contrary, or at least ..."

"What?"

"Brad was ... clever. I would guess he never stepped outside the law in any way, but he knew how to keep his balance just at the edge of the divide. And he had no scruples about turning regulations around on people. He got after one bed-and-breakfast owner I know to put fire doors in her Victorian house, which would have ruined the structure. Luckily, Jane was able to get the building listed on the historic register before she actually had to do the renovations."

"Could she have held a grudge?"

"Oh, no. Jane's a let's-get-on-with-it kind of person. She doesn't dwell on the past. Not that she ever spoke to Brad again that I know of, but she didn't talk about him behind his back either. Of course, he may have resented *her.* I'd guess that he preferred being hated to being dismissed."

"Anyone else?"

She thought about that, and sighed. So many people resented Brad, or openly disliked him. They were people whose motives she had never questioned before; in some cases she scarcely knew them well enough to guess at what drove them. But were any of them capable of murder? She supposed that in a fit of rage, even people she had known for years were capable of violence. But murder?

Suddenly she realized that the word didn't appall her anymore. She glanced accusingly at Alex, but he was watching her from across the table with that hint of amusement in his eyes. *Sexy amusement*, she thought. Damn him. She knew she was easily manipulated, easily led down any path a friendly hand took her, but knowledge of her own frailties was no comfort.

"Is there anything else you'd like?" she said, standing up abruptly. "To eat or drink, I mean." She picked up the teapot and his mug and looked at him as if daring to ask for anything else. But again, he caught her off guard.

"I don't suppose you'd like to show me the scene of the crime?" he asked, as if he was unaware of the direction her thoughts had taken and her evasive maneuvers. That was the disadvantage of a fair complexion; she blushed far too visibly, even in the dim light of the kitchen.

"Not particularly," she responded. She put the mugs in the sink and put her hand on the kettle on the counter; almost cold. She didn't offer to turn it on, but began clearing the cake plates.

"Well, it's a public place, I understand. I daresay I could find it myself. It would be the cemetery next to the Town Hall, wouldn't it?" He rose as if prepared to set off immediately.

"You're not really going to go over there with your deerstalker and magnifying glass, are you?"

"I'll leave the hat behind if you think I'll be ridiculed."

"I don't suppose you care if you are."

"Again, it's part of what I do for a living."

It occurred to her that what he did for a living was both more personal and more objective than she had imagined. That made it difficult to tell where the real Alex Gordon left off and the part took over—or even what part he might be playing at any given time. She could not recall seeing, in any of his performances, the kind of playful humor he displayed now. She couldn't help envying him for that.

"What is it you are acting in this season, apart from *Romeo and Juliet?*" she asked, only partly to keep him from making off down the Green on his own.

"That role is what you might call a cameo," he said, not at all put off by her seeming non sequitur. "I'll be playing the Prince, a mere walk-on at the beginning and the end. I expect they asked me to do it because I'm too old for any of the other parts—even Juliet's father—and they don't want me cooling my expensive heels before *Duchess* opens."

She knew better. The festival's director, Mark Edwards, had told her when he first contacted Alex Gordon that he would be a draw even in a "cameo" part. The production, which otherwise was cast with unknowns, needed the publicity. She did not think Alex was so disingenuous as to not know this also, but at least she was beginning to recognize when she should not snap at his bait.

She said instead, "So they're definitely doing *The Duchess of Malfi?* I was told that some board members thought no one would come to see it."

"Apparently the season ticket holders will come to anything."

"They didn't to *Timon of Athens* last year."

"That's because I wasn't in it. After I've been the best Duke Ferdinand since Eric Porter. I'll attack *Timon* too."

"That's the first sign of ego you've let slip."

"You didn't really think I had none, did you?"

"I assumed you had, but..." She was going to say that the best actors she had ever met had the least ego, but that might sound more like flattery than she meant to convey. She thought she had best not say anything rather than say something he'd doubtless remember and tease her about later.

He didn't seem to mind the silence either, or the awkwardness of their both standing there with no particular purpose. He pulled out the plug to the kettle, as if to tell her that he knew she had had enough of him. She said nothing, watching the movement of his large laborer's hands.

"Am I keeping you from your bed?" he asked finally.

"What? Oh ... no." She hadn't been thinking of that at all. In fact, she was wide awake now. "What time is it?"

"'The dappled dawn doth rise,'" he said, glancing out the window. When she frowned, he looked pleased and said, "Milton."

She smiled but turned her head toward the kitchen clock. Half past six. "I suppose there's not much point going to bed now anyway."

"Shall we go for a walk, then?"

She caught that mischievous glint in his blue eyes—which looked remarkably clear and wide awake considering the hour.

Still, she could not help responding. She said, "Which may just happen to take us past Town Hall and the old burying ground?"

"Only if you lead the way. I don't know the town, remember."

"It hasn't changed much in fifteen years—and the town knows you well enough, I suspect."

Chapter 9

It was light enough outside to walk without difficulty when they set out, and the street lamps on the Green turned themselves off as they approached the graveyard. At the sight of the yellow police markers, Diana hesitated.

"Steady on," Alex said, taking her elbow. "There are no ghosts there now."

"That's what you think," she said, but felt stronger for the pressure on her arm. "Why do those tapes say 'Crime Scene'? It's supposed to have been an accident."

"I'm not sure," he admitted. "It may be that it remains an unexplained death until the autopsy is done, at which time the scene needn't be protected from clumsy civilians who will tread on all the evidence."

"Like us."

He grinned. "Or it may just be that your local constabulary doesn't have any other kind of tape to hand."

"Thank you, Sherlock," she retorted. "That was insightful."

He held aside the yellow plastic ribbon as if it were a velvet rope guarding the entrance to the best box seat in the theater, and she bowed graciously on her way through.

"*That* was very royal," he said, following her down the path.

"I saw the queen do it once."

"More than I have, I regret to say. I've been waiting for my O.B.E. for years."

"I expect you have to be a rock musician to get one."

This silliness diverted her mind until they came to the spot where she had found Brad's body. Now, however, in the light of almost-day, there was nothing to see but a little flattened grass where the police had trampled it.

"This is it," she said, then added, as if she were seeing the graveyard through new eyes, "It looks ... normal." It was a relief to realize how normal it was.

He looked around interestedly just the same. "What did they say happened?"

"He seemed to have slipped in the mud there"— Diana pointed to the path leading toward Town Hall— "and hit his head on this marker." There were faintly visible streaks in the mud to the side of the gravel path, as if to confirm this hypothesis. It hadn't rained for several days, so any marks Brad might have made would still be visible—if they hadn't, as Alex pointed out, been trod on by the police and any subsequent, unknown investigators. Diana made a mental note to ask Beth Hudson if she or any of her staff had been there in pursuit of a news story.

Alex studied the headstone she pointed out. He might as well have a magnifying glass, she thought, wondering what he could see that she could not.

Nothing much, apparently. He said, "I don't see any blood."

"The police must have taken it away," she said, drawing a puzzled look from him. She pointed.

"There's a piece missing—see? Any blood would have been on that."

He looked. "It's *marble,* for God's sake. He must have had a very hard head to have broken anything off."

"Actually," Diana said, "Marble isn't as hard as you might think. And it doesn't age well. It was commonly used in the eighteenth century for monuments, especially in New England, with all the quarries we have, but after the Civil War, granite was more usual. It's harder and lasts longer."

She looked on as he inspected the broken corner, noting that the unadorned stone belonged to one Marcus Gray, 1782-1847, presumably one of Bradford Gray's less illustrious ancestors, unworthy of expensive carving and noble sentiments. Alex looked down the slight slope the path took in the direction of Town Hall.

"Would he have been coming up the path or down when he fell? It's not much of a slope, but surely he would have slid *down*, not sideways onto the verge. I don't see any marks."

Diana looked back toward the gate they had entered by. There were so many footprints there that there was no way to distinguish Brad's. "Perhaps, in a struggle to keep his balance, he propelled himself upwards," she said, looking down the slope again and trying unsuccessfully to visualize the scene. At least it was no longer horror at the blood she had glimpsed on Brad's body that shut down her imagination, only ignorance about what to look for at an accident scene. "Otherwise, he might have fallen onto that slab over there."

"And if he hit his head there"—Alex pointed to Marcus Gray's stone—"why did he fall so far away?" He took two long steps up to the plinth. "Here."

"I don't know."

"What did the police think he did?"

"I didn't ask for details."

The gate creaked just then, and Diana jumped. He took her arm again, and she relaxed almost at once. It was uncanny, the effect he had on her—soothing and exciting at the same time.

"Who's that?" he asked.

Diana looked. "It's the police in person. Chief Brewster. You can ask your questions yourself."

Kent was out of uniform, apparently off duty, and looking tired. He appeared not to see them as he began rolling up the yellow tape, but as he approached, he remarked conversationally, "Up early, Diana, aren't you?" He glanced at Alex, whose expression was blandly agreeable. "Or haven't you been to bed?"

"Mrs. Quick was upset about the—er, incident last night," Alex said apologetically. "We thought that visiting the scene by daylight might help."

Diana said quickly, "You said you wanted to talk to me today, Kent."

"Yes, but I was figuring on your coming to the office this afternoon."

Kent glanced again at Alex, and Diana belatedly introduced the two men. Kent didn't seem overly impressed by Alex's name, but Diana knew he had never had much interest in the theater festival, except in how it affected his job. Many Middlefordians worked at jobs in some way connected with the festival, but a sizable minority took no interest, never attended a performance, and griped about not being able to get in and out of the IGA in under half an hour in the summer. This minority, Mark Edwards complained, was the bane of his existence, but he'd given up trying to convert them.

Kent took a neutral stand somewhere above the no-shows. His wife, Larraine, was a supporter of the festival, and he attended opening nights with her when he wasn't working.

"Well," he said, "as you see, Diana, it looks just like it did yesterday, as if nothing happened. Marjorie tells me the funeral will be on Friday, by the way, if you plan to go."

"Thanks," she said. "I will. I should pay a call on Marjorie as well. How is she?"

Kent shrugged. "She's holding up."

Diana interpreted this to mean that Marjorie Bradford was enjoying the attention she received as a tragically sudden widow, but she said nothing. She did not believe in speaking badly of anyone behind her back, even Marjorie, who avoided her whenever possible. Daniel had said once that Marjorie was jealous of Diana's real glitter, as opposed to Marjorie's fake gilding. He had been making a joke, but there was a grain of truth in it. Marjorie—who refused to answer to "Marge"—had never known how to treat Diana, who was neither superior nor inferior to her, yet they were somehow not on the same level.

"Chief, can you tell me what exactly happened here?"

Kent eyed Alex suspiciously. "What's your interest in this?"

Alex smiled ingratiatingly. "I suppose I'm just curious—morbidly so, perhaps, but believe it or not, I once took a course in criminology, and I've always been fascinated by police work. I'm well aware that you do a much more valuable job than I do."

The patent flattery softened Kent enough to disregard the implication that a crime had been committed. Diana guessed he had sometimes felt unappreciated, like an old easy chair. Comfortable but not something one showed off to company. She was sometimes guilty of thinking of him that way herself. She certainly could not remember the last time she'd asked his opinion about anything.

"Well," he said, and then repeated the same theory Diana had given Alex about the muddy path and the broken tombstone. Alex nodded encouragingly and did not interrupt.

"I don't see the broken piece anywhere," he observed when Kent came to the end of his account.

"We removed it from the scene. Some curiosity seeker might easily have picked it up, and we can't have that."

"Why? Do you mean you're going to have tests done on it?"

Kent looked mildly startled. "What tests?"

"I don't know," Alex admitted. "Blood tests? To see if it was really the victim's—that is, the deceased's blood on the stone? Even just to see if the wound matches the shape of the marble?"

Kent was running out of tolerance. "Mr. Gordon, I appreciate your interest, but it's not customary to run forensic tests in the case of accidental death. You not being a taxpayer in this town might not consider this."

"So you're certain it was an accident? Has the autopsy been concluded already?"

Kent scowled. "Not formally. But Doc Sunderland was pretty firm about its being an accident, and I'll take his word for it." He seemed to suddenly notice the rolled-up tape in his hand and stuffed it into his jacket pocket. "What else could it have been, after all?"

Before Alex could answer that, Diana interrupted. "I imagine a full-scale investigation would run into money the town wouldn't be willing to spend to investigate a natural death."

"Well, it wasn't technically a natural death," Kent conceded. "That's why an autopsy's being done at all. Maybe even some blood tests," he added in Alex's direction. "But I'm confident that the M.E.'s formal ruling will match Sunderland's conclusion at the time— accidental death by a fall against the tombstone."

"I daresay," Alex murmured, gazing thoughtfully at the tombstone in question. "It couldn't have happened any other way, you don't suppose?"

"Just what are you trying to imply, Mr. Gordon?" Kent asked testily. "If you have any information—"

Alex turned his famous smile on Kent. "I do beg your pardon, Chief. I assure you, I'm implying nothing—certainly no slur against the Middleford police department's professionalism. I speak from mere idle curiosity."

"Are you going to be starring in any of the festival productions this season, Mr. Gordon?" Kent asked, apparently out of the blue.

"Yes, I am."

"Good. Then I suggest you get on with rehearsing, or whatever your work consists of these days, and don't waste your time, or mine, speculating on a tragedy that can mean nothing to you, but does matter a great deal to Middleford."

"Kent, I'm sure Mr. Gordon means no disrespect," Diana began in an attempt to mollify him. Alex *had* been insensitive, but he didn't know that Kent and Brad had been friends.

"As for you, Diana, I'd discourage your guest, if that is what he is, from poking his nose in what doesn't concern him and possibly raising a stink that I'd have a hell of a time cleaning up. Besides, if you think about it, if Brad's death wasn't an accident, you could be the first person suspicion falls on."

"On me?" she repeated, astonished.

"You were the one who discovered the body. I imagine you would have been the only other person anyone saw in the vicinity of the graveyard after eight o'clock. If anyone had seen anything."

Alex raised an eyebrow at her, as if she had been keeping valuable information from D.C. Dickson. She ignored him. "But what reason could I possibly have had—even if I could physically have done it?"

"Hadn't Brad been a thorn in your side about the inn for years? Suppose he had succeeded in blocking your plans? How much would that have cost you? How much would that have just plain pissed you off?"

"Kent, you know that's absurd."

The chief's expression relaxed visibly, and his posture lost its tension. "Of course, it is. I'm sorry, Diana. I didn't mean to lose my temper. I guess I'm just tired. If you'll excuse me, I think I'd better go home and get some sleep."

He turned to Alex. "I apologize to you, too, Mr. Gordon. I'm sure your interest in Middleford affairs does you credit. If you really want to know the details, it will all be in the public record. Feel free to stop by my office tomorrow and I'll answer your questions. The autopsy report should be in by then."

"Thank you, Chief. I'll try not to be a nuisance."

Kent looked at him as if he doubted he could help it, but said nothing and walked out the gate, yanking the rest of the yellow plastic tape off the shrubbery as he went, then stuffing it into the trash bin on the sidewalk outside as he passed.

Diana looked at Alex. "You—"

"Don't say it. No doubt I was crude and unfeeling, and I'm probably barking up the wrong tree. But it worked, didn't it?"

"What do you mean?"

He smiled. "You don't look shell-shocked anymore. I'd rather you weren't angry with me instead, but it's a start. I'll work on sweetening you up later."

"Do you mean to say, you deliberately engineered this little field trip to take my mind off finding the body?"

"Maybe." He took her elbow to escort her up the path, but paused to give the scene one last look, taking in the path, the muddy grass, and the broken tombstone.

"But now," he added, "I'm interested too."

Chapter 10

Bradford Gray's funeral was the social event of the season, outdrawing even the festival's most recent opening night. This year's was only two weeks away and might well pale by comparison, Diana thought. Most of Middleford was there, including many people Diana did not know even by sight. She supposed they were business associates of Brad's, or even theatrical people there for the show, though she recognized none of them.

It was an appropriate day for a funeral. It had rained overnight and the sky was still gray, with the occasional bank of scudding clouds threatening to pour on the burial later. At least the cemetery was just behind the church and protected by a high wall and numerous trees.

St. James's Episcopal Church was an elegant stone building at the opposite end of the green from the white clapboard Congregational Church, where generations of her family and Daniel's had been christened, married, and buried. Brad's had, too, but when he married Marjorie, she had convinced him that the Anglican service was more dignified than the Congregational and therefore more in keeping with the Grays' social standing in the community. Diana had become accustomed to Church of England services living in England, although she had never mentioned that to Marjorie, and so she was equally comfortable in either church.

The organist was playing Albinoni's *Adagio*—quite well, Diana noted with pleasure—when she entered the cool, dry interior of the church, but the service had not yet formally begun. She took a pew to the rear, where she could observe the attendees unobserved herself, and glanced around the sanctuary. Nigel had offered to escort Diana, but she had declined this sacrifice on his part in favor of undistracted study of the players in this particular pageant.

Her first impression was that there were more women present than men, a testament perhaps to Brad's vaunted charm. None of them seemed to display any emotion but curiosity, and she could scarcely fault anyone for that; it was her own motive in coming.

Diana was dressed in regulation black and a small hat, but several other women wore pastel colors, as if this were a bridge party or they were on their way to one as soon as this tiresome obligation was out of the way. Their male escorts congregated together, probably discussing business rather than Brad—or Brad's business and what would happen to it now. Ben McIlvey was even now the center of the largest male conclave.

The widow sat in a front pew. Diana had seen her come in, stylishly dressed in a severely cut black suit, with a wide-brimmed black hat and veil. Her head had been bowed, and she clutched a handkerchief in her black-gloved hand, as if to wipe away tears. For a moment Diana wondered if Marjorie Gray really was devastated by her husband's death—until someone slipped into the pew beside her and whispered, "I hear she just had her second facelift and it hasn't had time to heal. If Brad weren't already dead, she'd kill him for making her come out of the house before next week."

Jane Wagner, proprietress of Willow Lane Cottage, the bed-and-breakfast Diana had told Alex about, was no friend of the deceased either. But she had known Marjorie Gray (née Bonning) when she was an unspoiled—or at least pre-cosmetically altered— teenager.

"She's fifty if she's a day," Jane whispered, sitting down next to Diana in her pew, "and if she has another facelift, everyone will know it."

"I didn't know she'd had *one* facelift," Diana whispered back.

"You just don't care," Jane said. "I swear, Diana, I've never met anyone as uninterested in gossip as you are. You're no fun at all."

Diana smiled. If Jane only knew how she'd taken to digging the dirt lately! She said, "Daniel used to say that after a certain age, some women fix up well."

Jane gave a strangled version of her usually hearty laugh and looked around to see if anyone had heard. "Daniel," she whispered, "was never fooled by anyone."

Diana thought about that and realized that Jane was right. She, on the other hand, always took people at face value, literally and figuratively, and was inevitably hurt when they did not live up to the image she had formed of them. Daniel had told her fondly that this was her most endearing quality, but she had always thought it was not a life skill that came in very useful. Not if one did not have a Daniel there to soothe her hurts.

For no reason that she cared to think about, her mind went back to Alex Gordon. It was because he had planted the idea of murder in her mind—she was beginning to accept that word without cringing—that she was here today. If it were true that in crimes of this sort, the murderer invariably turned up at the funeral of his victim, she wanted to observe what she supposed she must begin thinking of as the suspects. Of course, most of Middleford's permanent residents were present in the church, so this would not appreciably narrow the field. Nor would the fact that almost everyone who knew Brad had some grudge against him.

Kent Brewster had gotten up to press Marjorie's hand and whisper something to her. Kent's wife, Larraine, remained in their pew, looking, it seemed to Diana, as if she would get up only if absolutely forced to. Larraine was a sweet, generous woman, one of the rare ones who grew more beautiful with age—and without the need for facelifts—but Diana knew she had her limits as far as charity went, and Marjorie was beyond them.

Diana hadn't talked to Kent since she saw him in the burying ground early in the morning two days ago. She hadn't even talked much to Alex, who was involved in rehearsals for *Romeo and Juliet.* He had, however, stopped in the night before to talk and prod more information out of her about Brad's associates.

"You see," he had said after she produced a further list of names, "you are coming around to my way of thinking."

"I'm not," she'd protested, not very convincingly. "It's just that Brad was such a—"

"Target?"

"Yes."

She had meant to say "mischief-maker," but Alex was looking at him from a different perspective. Diana now wondered if Brad had been aware of this. He must have been delighted to make trouble for people he disliked. No, not disliked—people he wanted to feel superior to. And that, again, was almost the entire population of Middleford.

Diana glanced at Ben McIlvey again. If there was ever anyone it was easy for Brad to look down on, it was Ben, who practically abased himself whenever Brad looked his way. At the moment, Ben was staring at the carved cherubs on the ceiling, as if considering their architectural function. He didn't look capable of murder, but then, one could supposedly never tell. Perhaps Brad had stepped on him once too often; perhaps the worm had turned.

Now why had she thought of that? Alex Gordon had been putting ideas into her mind about people she had known all her life, ideas that would never have occurred to her if Brad hadn't died and Alex hadn't entered her life on the same day.

The vicar stepped solemnly up to the pulpit at that moment, and the low murmur of voices in the church ceased as he began reading from the Book of Common Prayer. For a few moments, Diana became caught up in the beauty of the words. Reverend Hawley had a mellifluous voice, and even Jane, beside her, listened attentively. In the front row, Marjorie Gray bowed her head and held her black-gloved hand to her mouth.

"Lord, thou has been our refuge, from one generation to another...."

Diana wondered again about Marjorie. She had never gotten to know Brad's wife, who had grown up in Middleford but had lived out of state when she was married to her first husband—Brad was her second—and returned only after Diana had married and moved away herself. They were not all that far apart in age and shared childhood experiences, yet their paths had rarely crossed. Diana decided that she would have to make a detour and reintroduce herself to Marjorie.

"For man walketh in a vain shadow, and disquieteth himself in vain; he heapeth up riches and cannot tell who shall gather them...."

Diana's attention was jerked forcibly back to what Reverend Hawley was saying. Was it her imagination or was he choosing far too accurately the parts of the psalms that applied uniquely to Brad?

Apparently this had occurred to other people, because an almost imperceptible shiver went through the congregation. Kent Brewster looked up, scowling. Jane grinned, then hid her face in a hymnal. Beth Hudson, also in a rear pew, surreptitiously pulled a notepad out of her purse. Ben McIlvey ceased his contemplation of the wood scrolling on the pews and frowned—not, Diana guessed, because he had been listening, but at the reaction of some of the other attendees.

Who benefits? Wasn't that the first question one asked about a motive for crime? Marjorie would presumably benefit, through insurance or Brad's will, but surely she had had more money than she needed before Brad's death, unless ... Diana admitted that she had no idea of how Marjorie spent her money or how she might get into irretrievable debt. Jane was right; she had never been very curious about that kind of thing. She would have to develop her curiosity.

Ben would benefit too, surely. He would take over the lucrative business he owned in partnership with Brad, and the profits as well. And he would be able to run the business as he saw fit instead of being forever Brad's second fiddle. How much had that bothered Ben?

But Ben had been at the zoning meeting when she arrived at Town Hall that night, before she found the body. But when exactly *was* Brad killed? Would that be in the autopsy report?

The congregation rose for the hymn and were soon parading slowly out of the church behind the coffin, toward the cemetery behind the church. It was, Diana thought as she followed the casket as unobtrusively as possible, an undeniably peaceful setting. More dramatic than the ancient burying ground near the Town Hall, it was dominated by tall cypresses, and the grass was so neatly kept that she hesitated to step on it.

The procession—Kent Brewster was one of the pallbearers, Diana noted, although Ben McIlvey wasn't—filed down a short gravel path toward an open grave under a green-and-white canopy at the bottom of a slight rise. Reverend Hawley took Marjorie's arm and led her to a chair, then waited with her until the coffin was in place before he began his final prayers. Everyone listened avidly.

But any further insights the minister might have offered gave way to the customary words of comfort to the living.

"Thou shalt show me the path of life; in thy presence is the fullness of joy, and at thy right hand there is pleasure for evermore…."

For a moment, Diana felt herself being carried away again on the music of the words. A moment later, she wished she had a copy of the Book of Common Prayer to look in for the context of the words that seemed to ring in her ears.

"Thou knowest, Lord, the secrets of our hearts," Reverend Hawley went on. "Shut not thy merciful ears to our prayer, Lord most holy; suffer us not, at our last hour, for any pains of death, to fall from thee."

Diana looked around, but no one else seemed to find any hidden meaning in this, any reference to what they thought of Brad, of how he died.

Her imagination was working overtime again, that was all.

Nonetheless, she looked around her to see who might be harboring secrets in their hearts. Marjorie could have been, but her veil hid anything her expression might reveal, and she was probably expert at hiding her feelings. Ben McIlvey didn't look as if he were listening. She suspected that he wouldn't have found any hidden meaning in the words anyway; Ben wasn't that devious. Seth Howell and his daughter, Cynthia, stood next to Ben, but not with him. Seth looked resigned; Cynthia only interested. Diana wondered if this was the first funeral she'd ever attended. Her mother, Seth's late wife, had died when Cynthia was a child, so perhaps Seth had sheltered her from such sadness as best he could.

Mildred Goodall, standing off to the side beside her husband Andrew, on the other hand, was quietly crying. Diana knew of the Goodalls only that they, like so many other Middleford residents, had clashed with Brad over some zoning matter. So why was Mildred crying at Brad's funeral? Farther back, Mark Edwards was also watching Mildred, his face impassive. Mark had been an actor before he became artistic head of the Festival, so his expression meant nothing; but why was he there?

Diana sighed and returned her attention to the conclusion of the service.

"The God of peace, who brought again from the dead our Lord Jesus Christ," Reverend Hawley read in a low tone, "make you perfect in every good work to do his will, working in you that which is well pleasing in his sight; through Jesus Christ, to whom be glory for ever and ever."

The mourners murmured "amen," and the minister closed his book, spoke a few more whispered words to Marjorie, and led her away from the grave. At this implicit signal, the rest of the mourners followed slowly, speaking among themselves softly at first, then as they neared the gate, more loudly, like children released from class, glad to have this ordeal over and done.

Diana remained where she was for a moment, thinking. *In every good work to do his will ...* What was she thinking? Was this any of her business? Who would benefit from her meddling? What sort of "good work" could it be, and what good could she do?

She turned to leave, following Kent and Larraine Brewster out of the cemetery. Kent's cell phone buzzed just at that moment—he'd put it on vibrate during the service, but she was close enough to hear it—and he opened it up, his left hand still holding Larraine's. He paused, listened for a moment, then closed the phone and whispered something to Larraine. She nodded and waved him off. Police business, Diana supposed. An emergency, from the look of it. She wondered what it might be.

Beth Hudson, her notebook out in plain view, heard as well, but did not try to catch up with Kent, who was walking swiftly toward his car, and approached Diana instead.

"Larraine was crying," she said, "so I didn't do my intrusive, big-city reporter number." Diana must have looked skeptical, because she added, "Besides, I can find out what it was by my scanner later."

She paused, as if waiting for a response, but Diana didn't have one. Beth went on, "So *is* there any question about how Brad died?"

"What?" Startled, Diana stared at Beth, who seemed to find her reaction sufficient answer to her question and made a note.

"Wait a minute," Diana said. "Where did you get that idea?"

"I had an anonymous tip."

Diana managed not to blurt out Alex's name and hoped she did not show her annoyance in her face.

"What did this anonymous tipper say, exactly?"

"Unfortunately, I didn't speak to him. He left a message on my Voice Mail, saying only that so many people disliked Brad that it was amazing that he died a natural death."

"That sounds like an impolite editorial, not a story."

"I'm not planning to start printing anonymous tips, but the observation was true enough. You found the body, Diana—was there anything about it to indicate foul play?"

She talked as if Diana was as detached about it as a policeman—or a reporter—might be, but somehow this worked to suppress her imagination and stimulate her reason. It did not, however, make her less cautious in her reply.

"Like what?"

"Well—wounds other than on his head, for example."

"Not that I noticed."

"Was the body still warm when you touched it? Was it soft or stiff?"

Diana winced, but said, "It felt like a—a sack of peat moss."

"Really!" Beth made a note. Diana cursed her lack of knowledge about rigor mortis. Here she had been wondering exactly when Brad died and she had a unique means of finding out. She would have to talk to Dr. Sunderland, who besides now being a part-time medical examiner after his retirement from practice, had been her family physician for years.

"Did you—" Beth began again.

"Beth, I'm sorry, but I have to get home now. Can you call me later today?"

"Could I come over? I meant to on Thursday—you know, we talked about it after the meeting, but then this story broke and I never got to it. After five, I think you said?"

"Sure." Diana couldn't think of a reason not to invite her. If Alex were there, maybe Beth would realize who had made that anonymous call, and Alex would have to get out of the hole he'd dug himself into on his own.

On the other hand, although Beth was a good reporter, Alex was a great actor. If he had wanted to disguise his voice, he would have done it right.

"But make it Sunday, if you can, after six," she told Beth. "The house will be quieter then, with everyone at rehearsals." Including Alex, most likely, but she didn't really want that confrontation in her house.

And she needed today to confront Alex and ask him what he thought he was up to.

Chapter 11

Diana arrived home, having worked herself up into righteous indignation over Alex's meddling, only to find him oblivious to her mood. He and Nigel were sitting on two of the white wicker chairs on the verandah, drinking iced tea and reading their scripts. Alex was apparently cuing Nigel on his lines for *Romeo and Juliet,* but she heard only a few words before they caught sight of her and abruptly stopped.

Both of them rose to their feet, apparently delighted to see her. Nigel offered his chair, then drew another up to the small round table that held their drinks. She smiled warmly at him, ignoring Alex, who raised his eyebrows but said nothing.

"I'll get you some tea," Nigel said, when she'd sat down, and darted off.

"Thank you, dear," Diana said to his departing back. Alex's brows rose another fraction of an inch, then fell again as he smiled, amused but apparently unwilling to invite her to unburden herself of whatever grievance she was harboring.

"You look very elegant," he observed instead as she crossed her black-hosed legs and put her black clutch on the patio table they'd been using. She took off her hat and shook out her hair, disregarding his comment, although it pleased her enough that she had to hide a smile. She was determined not to be cajoled out of her annoyance with him.

"How was it?" he asked politely.

"What do you mean, how was it?" she asked. "It was a *funeral*."

"It's not as if you were—ah, intimate with the deceased."

"Perhaps not, but someone was, or was at least sorry that he died."

"Who?"

He asked the question almost eagerly, and it suddenly struck Diana that it was a terrible thing to realize, that Brad had no friends, that no one cared that he was gone, even, to all appearances, his wife. She sent up a small, belated prayer that she would not leave behind such emptiness when her time came.

As if he had sensed her thoughts, Alex reached out and squeezed her hand. For a moment, she accepted his touch. Then she drew a deep breath and said, "What were you thinking, leaving anonymous tips for the local paper?"

"How did you know it was me?"

"Who else would it have been?"

"I'd have thought that speculating on that question, rather than leaping to conclusions, would have been a useful exercise."

"I'd already speculated quite enough to exercise my brain."

"And what was the result?"

She hesitated, thinking again that she could be sorry for Brad if she put her mind to it. Nigel returned, bearing fresh iced tea for them all. Diana stayed long enough to drink half a glass and chat desultorily about how rehearsals were going, then rose to go. The men, ever gentlemen despite her petulance, began to stand.

"Don't get up," she said. "I'm just going to change. You can get back to your work."

Neither of them made any move to stop her, but an hour later Alex found her in the kitchen. She had changed into jeans and a T-shirt and was stacking the morning's breakfast dishes in the dishwasher. He silently began helping, handing her the dishes piled in the sink for transfer to the machine.

"I thought you had help for this kind of thing," he said when they'd finished and she had shoved the washer door closed and turned the machine on.

"I do, but I gave her the day off. Sometimes housework helps me to think." She smiled. "Most times, though, it just makes me tired. Did you want something? To eat, I mean?"

"No, thanks. I just came to find out what you've been thinking about. You obviously had something more on your mind than you told us when you returned from the funeral."

She put a bowl of fresh fruit on the kitchen table, then sat down and indicated that he should take the chair opposite her. They were already in the cozy habit of talking over the kitchen table—how had that happened? Diana supposed it was safer than some other places, but in a way it was even more intimate.

He had used that word earlier, but she couldn't remember when. She frowned.

"You aren't still cross about my calling the newspaper, are you?" he prompted.

"No, I suppose not. If we're going to investigate what you're pleased to think of as a crime, I suppose any help would be useful, and Beth Hudson is the logical person to go about asking questions."

She looked at him. "How exactly were you going to get her to tell us whatever she finds out? You being anonymous and all."

He smiled. "I was hoping we could work out a—well, a sort of plan."

"What sort of a plan?"

"Tell me first what you observed at the funeral."

Not sure if she had observed anything useful, she gave him a summary of what had happened, who had been there, and what Jane and Beth had said to her. She kept her feelings about Reverend Hawley's choices of liturgy to herself. It must just have been guilt on her part that she was even considering taking on this underhanded "investigation" that had prompted her interpretation.

"It won't be necessary, you know, to interview the suspects personally," he said, with an uncomfortably accurate reading of her mind. "The police can do that once we come up with a reason that Mr. Gray's death might have been more than a simple accident."

"You already hinted that to Kent Brewster the other night, and he told you off pretty effectively."

He grinned. "Hardly effectively. Anyone can tell me off, but there aren't too many critics I'll listen to. My hide's tougher than that."

"Don't tell me—it's part of your job."

He laughed, then leaned forward and said, "There are other ways to go about it."

To maintain her distance, she took some grapes out of the fruit bowl and leaned back as she ate them. "Such as?"

"Well, we've set Ms. Hudson on the trail. She'll do some legwork, and I expect I can offer myself as an interview subject for an entirely different—but legitimate— reason and coax the information we want out of her."

"I daresay you could," she observed wryly, hoping Beth, a thirty-something single woman, could weather his charm.

"Meanwhile," he went on blithely, "you could talk to your friend the police chief and find out what the autopsy report said."

"How am I supposed to do that? What makes you think there is an autopsy report anyway? Or that we can get access to it?"

"There is always an autopsy in cases of sudden or accidental death, remember?"

"Oh. Well, if you knew that, you can find out what's in the report too. I'm sure you can *coax* the information out of Doris Mallory."

"Who's that?"

"The town clerk. If there's a document that's available to the public, she'd know where to find it."

He stopped making mental notes and took out a small leather-bound notebook. Extracting a stubby pencil, he wrote Doris's name in the notebook.

"That's two chores for me," he said. "What *are* you willing to take on?"

She remembered Jane Wagner's eagerness to gossip and told him about it.

"Good. She may know something she doesn't know she knows."

She had to smile. "That does sound like D.C. Dickson."

He sounded aggrieved when he said, "You know, the character *was* promoted several times. He was a Detective Constable only for the first two seasons. He'd have made Inspector if the show had gone on another year."

"D.I. Dickson doesn't have the same ring," she teased.

"I suppose not," he conceded. "But I owe a lot to the boy, and I still feel a certain responsibility towards him."

"Is that why you've developed this sudden interest in detecting?"

"It's not so sudden. I got to know quite a few real policemen while I was doing the series, and got interested in their work. If I hadn't gone any further with my acting career, I was seriously thinking about police work as a fall-back."

"I think I see you more as a private eye."

"Only if I could live rent-free on an estate in Hawaii or a Fifth Avenue penthouse," he countered. "And perfect my American accent. In England, only American PI's get any respect."

She could sense that he was leading her down a conversational path that might be enjoyable, but that would deter them from their original goal. If she couldn't be disinterested, she could at least be businesslike.

"What else would Dickson do in this case?"

"Check on everyone's alibis, I suppose." He looked at her much the way Seth Howell did when he was prodding a permit applicant for an answer to some question. "Does everyone have one?"

"I suppose we ought to make a list of sus—people who need to have one."

"Right," he said, licking the stub of his pencil the way she remembered Dickson doing. She laughed.

"I think we're a little more up-to-date now, Sherlock. Come with me."

She got up and led the way to her study, where her computer was set up and continually on, since she tried to enter any expenses and inn-related business matters as soon as they came up. The study had no windows, having been converted from a pantry, but Diana liked it that way; she wouldn't be tempted to daydream if there was no view.

She pulled a fresh thumb drive from a drawer and inserted it.

"We'd better keep this separate from the rest of my records. You never know who might stumble on it otherwise."

He pulled a chair up to the computer next to her and watched over her shoulder. She could smell the faint scent of his aftershave and wondered what time he had gotten up that morning. But as that line of thought threatened to lead into avenues she blushed to consider, she shook her head to clear it, and tried not to be aware of his proximity.

She quickly set up a table, labeling the first column "Suspects," the second "Alibis," and the third "Motives." Under the first, she listed Marjorie Gray and Ben McIlvey, then hesitated before adding Jane Wagner.

"McIlvey is the business partner. Isn't Wagner the woman you were going to pump for gossip?"

"Yes. It's not that I think she's guilty of anything, but she did have a run-in with Brad about her bed-and-breakfast. I told you about it."

"I remember. Who else tangled with him that way?"

"Well, I guess I could check the meeting minutes in Town Hall. Right now I can only think of Andrew and Mildred Goodall. She's a retired schoolteacher, and they both run a gift shop now. Andrew was on one of the town boards when he had a run-in with Brad. I wasn't living in Middleford at the time, so I'm not sure about the details, but everyone was still talking about the ruckus a year later."

"Can we find out what it was about?"

"I suppose it's on record too, if I can find a date. They were at the funeral as well."

"Who else was there? Any other possibilities?"

"Oh, dear—dozens of people, I suppose; I don't know half their relationships to Brad."

"Just put down the ones you do know about, even if you don't think they're guilty."

She added the Goodalls and, feeling impish, Mark Edwards.

"Very funny," he said.

"Well, Mark did have a regular annual tantrum about Brad's opposition to anything he wanted to do for the festival."

"In that case," he said, a little smugly, "you'd better put yourself on the list."

"Me? Why?"

"You remember what Chief Brewster said—you were the one to find the body. The implication was, it seemed to me, that only you knew what it really looked like when you first saw it. Besides that, Gray opposed you about the inn, didn't he? You're certainly a likely suspect for a first draft."

She stifled a further protest and wrote herself down.

"Now," he said, edging his chair a little closer. She glanced down and saw his knee inches from hers. She moved her leg as imperceptibly as she could. "Who else had a grudge against Mr. Popularity?"

She laughed, a little hollowly. "You've put your finger on the problem. Almost everyone in town did."

"Who else is on the zoning board?"

"Seth Howell, Jesse Connolly, and Bill Burnell."

"Write them down, oh, Lady High Executioner."

She shivered. "Don't talk like that. This isn't just summer entertainment." She stood up suddenly and paced the room, trying to get her imagination under control.

He waited, without comment, until she sat down again, and then said, "You're right. But you can't get too involved either. We do have a serious goal here, but don't think too much about the outcome or you'll give up."

"I suppose you learned that from your police friends, too."

"As a matter of fact, I did." When she was silent for a moment, he added, "If you don't want to go on with this, now's the time to call a halt."

"It's not that I *want* to do it, exactly. It's just that I can't get it out of my mind. Even if I erased all this"— she waved at the computer screen—"I'd still think about it."

"Then we'd better get on with it."

She sighed. "I suppose." Moving to the "Motives" column, she wrote under her name, "resented Brad delaying permission for renovations."

"That's not much of a motive," she said in her own defense.

"People have been killed for a lot less. Killers often act on the spur of the moment ... which brings us to opportunity, or 'Alibis' by your reckoning. Where were you on Saturday the 14th?"

"It was Wednesday, and I was at the zoning meeting. Unless ..."

"Right. Back to time of death. Back to the autopsy report."

"I guess that's an official document, which has to be recorded and should be available to the public. But what about motives and other alibis? How do we find out about those?"

"If this were England, everyone would have obligingly garrulous servants. But I'd still recommend going in by the back stairs, so to speak. Interview secretaries, clients, mail carriers—anyone who's observant but not normally noticed.

"In fact," he added, "I could probably get some actors to do the deed so no one would guess who's behind it."

She shuddered. "Certainly not. The fewer people who know about this little scheme, the better, as far as I'm concerned."

"But you're going to use Mizzes Hudson and Wagner."

"I don't have to tell them why I'm asking."

"You may have a tough time keeping it secret."

She conceded that this might be true, but defended both Beth and Jane as discreet and helpful in all matters.

"Nigel would help, too," he suggested.

"He has other things on his mind. You may be doing a walk-on opening night, but he has a major part."

"That's not to say he wouldn't be delighted to help you."

She turned and looked at him, puzzled. He smiled. "Don't you know that Nigel adores you?"

She felt herself blushing and turned her face away again. "Don't be absurd. It's only—a crush, at most. I'm old enough to be his mother."

"Now that *is* absurd. You're not like anyone's mother. And Nigel has excellent taste."

He said this in a low, seductive voice, with yet a hint of amusement in it, as if challenging her to defend herself. Instead, she added Nigel's name to the list of suspects and under "Motive" typed, "defending his lady's honor."

Alex laughed.

When he finally rose reluctantly and said he needed to get to the theater, she walked with him to the French windows in the back parlor and pointed out the path leading to the front gate. He paused for a moment, sizing up the ditch and mounds of dirt dug out of the back yard for the installation of the new septic tank.

"How long is this supposed to go on?" he asked.

"Romeo tells me he'll be done by the end of the week," she said, "although it will take a good while for the grass to grow back. I may have to get an extra gardener."

He was staring at her now. "*Romeo?*"

She laughed. "Sorry, I keep forgetting how funny that sounds. He's my plumber—Romeo Vitelli. You must have seen his truck."

"He didn't have his first name stenciled on it." He thought for a moment and asked, "Does he have any interest in the theater?"

"Actually, I think he likes opera better. He claims to be a true Neapolitan."

"Pity. I'll offer him two tickets to the opening of *R-and-J* anyway. I think he ought to be there, for his namesake's sake."

"I'm sure he'd be honored."

Alex said he'd bring the tickets back with him and present them personally so that the plumber couldn't turn them down, then said good-bye. She watched his quick, easy stride and admired the grace of his movements as he disappeared around the plumbing obstacles toward the Green. He'd obviously had more serious training in movement and the classical theater arts than he let on, with all his talk about his television character.

Then she realized that she had one advantage over him. His biography was much more readily available to her than hers was to him. She went back to her study and logged on to the Internet.

Chapter 12

Diana was still at the computer when she heard voices from the front of the house. Startled, she glanced at the clock—she'd been working for only half an hour, but she had been so deeply immersed that it seemed she'd never surface. She got up and opened the door, then heard, "Diana?"

Beth Hudson gave her a quizzical look from outside the French doors. Diana opened them to let her in. "Sorry. I didn't hear you."

"No problem. A couple of the chorus boys let me in the gate."

Diana led her into the study and was about to shut down the computer, then decided Beth might want to know what she'd found.

"I didn't know you were such a computer geek," Beth said as she glanced at the screen and added, "Oh. Everyone in town's been logging onto the Festival's site to check on our dashing leading man—me first. There's more if you just do a search, although I suspect very little of that is accurate."

Diana laughed. "Here I was thinking I could provide you with some background for an interview. I assume you're going to do one with Alex—Mr. Gordon?" She leaned over to log off the site she'd been perusing.

Beth flopped on the sofa opposite Diana's favorite wicker rocking chair and slung her capacious purse onto the cushion beside her. Today she was wearing an olive-green Blue Fish jumper over a yellow T-shirt and, as always, looked terrific despite the thrown-together style of her wardrobe and the perennial disarray of her curly dark hair. Diana offered a drink, and Beth asked for coffee, saying she still had work to do, however much she felt like a Jack Daniels, and needed to stay awake. The swimming-fish screen saver appeared just as Diana returned from the kitchen with a carafe and a plate of oatmeal cookies.

"Oh, yum," Beth said, greedily helping herself. "Did Margo make these?" she added between bites.

"Who else?" Diana answered. Her housekeeper was well known for her rapport with a baking sheet.

Beth eyed her over her cup. "Don't you cook?"

"Cook, yes; bake, no. Although I haven't had much time for either lately, what with getting the inn up and running."

Beth swallowed a second cookie and licked the crumbs off her lip. "Oh, gosh, thanks for the reminder. I almost forgot that I came here to get a story about that. How's it going? I see Vitelli's taken over the yard. Do you still think you can open this summer?"

"I'm afraid it's going to get worse before he finally fills the hole. But everything else is going well. All the repainting is done, and the electric is up to code. Nearly all the bedrooms are done, except for linens and the last decorative touches. I'll give you a tour before you leave."

Beth asked more questions, which Diana answered easily. They allowed her not only to brag a little about her work on the inn, but to refocus her own mind on what, before last Wednesday, had been her only obsession. She was considering literally sitting back and basking in her accomplishment when Beth said, "Let's do that tour now, before the light goes, if you don't mind."

She dug a camera out of her purse and stood up. "Besides," she said, taking another cookie off the plate as she moved toward the door, "there's something else I want to ask you about afterwards."

Diana led the way down the hall to the main part of the house, which was separated by a double door from her private quarters—study, bedroom, small kitchen, and large bath—at the back of the house, the side facing the gatehouse and Elm Street, which had once been the main road into Middleford. At the end of the hall was a small guest sitting room with a television, a sofa, and a pair of overstuffed armchairs. Diana explained that the room was meant to serve as a buffer between the business and private parts of the house.

"It's a little retreat, too, for any guests who want to get out of their rooms without getting too public. It's off limits to the actors, although as I explained, they'll be here all summer, even after I open for other guests."

"I love this sofa," Beth said, plopping down into the wide-wale corduroy cushions with a sigh. "What about next year? I mean, if the house is full of paying guests—we all hope—can the actors stay?"

"I haven't decided yet. I may let them use the gatehouse for another season, or some of them may want to work here part-time—continuing the construction and yard work, minding the reception desk, that sort of thing."

Diana headed for the door, and Beth hauled herself off the sofa to follow her down a hallway. They paused while Beth took photos of the area that would become the lobby and reception desk, including the wallpaper in a reproduction Federal-era design, and then Diana led her up the stairs to the second floor, where the guest rooms would be located.

"Lovely staircase," Beth commented, smoothing her hand along the banister as they climbed the wide, carpeted steps.

"Thanks," Diana said. "It's one of the original features of the inn that we've been able to restore almost exactly. It was the first project I wanted to tackle, in fact. I thought it would inspire me to go on, and so it has." She ran her hand lovingly along the smooth surface of the wood. Beth made a note of the story and took more photos.

In the upstairs bedrooms, Diana pointed out the features that were particularly designed for guests' comfort, but to her pleasant surprise, Beth seemed more interested in the restoration that had been done. The older the architectural feature, it seemed, the more Beth liked it. She was fascinated by the uneven line of the ceiling junction with the walls in some smaller rooms.

"Haven't you ever lived in an old house?" Diana asked, amused. "I thought you were a New England native."

"I am," Beth said, "but I grew up in the Boston suburbs. Efficient but soulless—although I didn't think so at the time, of course. It's only since I moved here and bought my little cottage that—hey, wait a minute. Who's interviewing whom here?"

They both laughed, and Diana found herself more inclined to show Beth the corners of the house that meant the most to her—the room that had been her father's nursery; her grandfather's study, where he'd written his sermons; the fireplace in one bedroom that had been in that same spot when her great-grandfather warmed himself at it.

"Your great-grandfather was Joshua Sedley, is that right?" Beth asked.

"Yes. *His* grandfather, also named Joshua, built the house, although the original building was much smaller, and his father, Josiah, expanded it and made it into a coaching inn. But his timing was off, and there were very few coaches still on the roads. Middleford was no longer on a major through road or railway route, but I guess Josiah didn't know about market research before he started his project. He finally had to close the inn, although the family continued living in the house. They couldn't keep up the whole thing, though, until my grandfather Matthew began restoring it, in a small way, in the 1950s."

"Your family was living here during the Civil War?"

"Oh, yes, during all the wars the country's been involved in, starting with the French and Indian. The house was rumored to be a stop on the Underground Railroad before the Civil War, but rumors like that abound in New England homes. Personally, I think it's too far north to have been of much use, although there's a crawl space in the basement that my grandmother claimed had been a hiding place."

Beth asked to see that. Diana pulled on a cardigan, took a flashlight out of a drawer, and showed it to her, although it turned out to be little more than a hole under the kitchen, with a dirt floor. Beth, however, did not look disappointed, so Diana told her that the house had also served as a convalescent hospital for wounded Civil War veterans, some of whom had died there.

Beth shivered. "Do you have any ghosts?"

Diana smiled. "Everyone asks that. I don't think so. At any rate, I've never seen one, and if we haven't disturbed them with all the work we've been doing lately, they must sleep soundly indeed."

They descended the back stairs, which formerly led up to the servants' quarters, Diana told her, and down to what had been an outdoor kitchen. They emerged on the back lawn, which was beginning to look normal at last, except for the raw dirt around the unfinished septic works. Jim Bishop, who took a special interest in the garden, had been doing a yeoman job. She told Beth about it.

"Very devoted of him, considering how busy the actors have been with rehearsals," Beth noted. She adjusted her digital camera and went on taking photos as they walked around. The sun was lower in the sky, but cast a warm light on the white walls.

"May I see the gatehouse?" Beth asked.

Diana hesitated, but there was no reason not to show it to her. Fortunately, there was little sign of Alex's presence when they walked in, other than a few playscripts scattered on the sofa. The closet and bathroom doors were discreetly closed, and Diana did not offer to open them, remaining standing in the doorway to point out the building's features. Beth did look mildly disappointed now.

When they returned to the study, she asked, "So is it true that Alex Gordon has taken up residence in your gatehouse?"

Diana was taken aback, less by the question than the reminder in Beth's use of the word 'residence' that Alex had originally asked to stay only a few days, until his rental house was ready for him. He hadn't mentioned it since the night he arrived. She wondered if she should ask.

"Temporarily, yes," she compromised, but Beth didn't miss her slight frown.

"How long is that?"

"Two weeks, I think he said. He got here early—to Middleford, I mean—and the owners weren't out of the house he had rented yet, so Enid Peterson sent him over here."

"Ah-hah ..." Beth made a note in her book, which Diana was reasonably certain read, *Call Enid P re AG rental.*

She told herself that there was no reason to make Beth's job easier by telling her things she could find out for herself. The official biography she had found on the

Internet revealed only that Alex had been born in Nova Scotia, trained as a classical actor in London, but became widely known through a television police drama. Since then he'd had an equally successful run in a series of movies featuring the same character. He'd said good-bye to Detective Constable Dickson to star in independent films and character parts, and was now returning to his theatrical roots.

The bio did not mention Alex Gordon's first brief, pre-D.C. Dickson appearance at the Middleford Festival in its opening season, but Middleford was well aware of it now, if not at the time, thanks to Mark Edwards's publicity office. Alex's official website also did not mention some of the details of his youth that he'd revealed to her, nor much about his one failed marriage, which he had not. Diana debated the merits of asking Beth to hunt up more information about this in exchange for an introduction to her celebrated guest. She decided against it, partly because Beth could doubtless get access to anyone at the Festival simply by asking, but more because she wasn't ready to reveal the extent of her own curiosity.

"Now," Beth went on, making herself comfortable on the sitting room sofa again when they had finished the tour, "what about this tip?"

"Tip?" Diana sat down at the other end of the sofa and looked at Beth, trying to decide if the conversational leap from Alex to that wretched anonymous tip was purely coincidental, or if Beth suspected who the tipper was. Apparently she didn't, Diana decided finally, for she went on in a no-nonsense tone that gave no indication of covert knowledge.

"The tip I got at the paper that Brad Gray's death may not have been accidental," Beth said, reaching for the last cookie as if it had been awaiting her return. "You found the body, Diana. I don't like to remind you of that—I'm sure it was an unpleasant experience—but do you remember thinking anything of the sort at the time? Was there anything about the scene that might suggest it? Did Kent or anyone else give any hint of a question?"

Diana shook her head. "I wasn't thinking very clearly at the time. In fact, I can scarcely remember what happened between the time I tripped over—over the body—and when the police showed up."

"Did you see anyone else, either before or after?"

"I don't remember seeing anyone—except Nigel, of course."

"Nigel Henson?" Beth made a note.

"He'd come to pick me up. That must have been just before ten, because we'd arranged to meet at Town Hall at ten. That's when I'd originally estimated that the meeting, or at least my part of it, would be over, and of course in the normal way—"

She stopped abruptly. She was babbling and knew it. She waited for Beth to ask another question.

"When was the last time you saw Brad?"

"I actually hadn't seen him for days. I think the last time was at the press conference at the theater announcing the guest list for opening night and the other events planned for that week."

"How did he seem to you?"

Diana shrugged. "I barely said hello to him. He seemed the same as usual."

In fact, now that she thought of it, Brad had been scowling, and she thought she remembered hearing his voice raised in the kind of single-minded tenor monotone he used when arguing with someone, as if plowing ahead with what he was saying, allowing no interruptions, would settle the argument, despite anything the other person might try to say. She supposed that was "the same as usual" as far as Brad was concerned. She wished she could remember who the other party to the dispute might have been.

"He didn't seem—well, pissed off at something?"

Diana glanced at her. "Why do you say that?"

Beth smiled. "No secret. Julia Desmond told me he'd been throwing his weight around. Any idea why?"

"No. I hadn't heard that," Diana answered, perfectly truthfully. She tried to remember if Julia had been at that press conference. She supposed she'd have to pump Jane for that bit of gossip too. What had the festival's leading lady, the usually gracious Julia Desmond, found to annoy her about Bradford Gray?

"Getting back to the night in question," Beth began, making Diana smile. There was D.C. Dickson again. But Beth apparently didn't realize she was parodying the character.

"Why do you suppose Brad was on foot?" she asked.

"I don't know—unless he had some sort of car trouble nearby, and it was easier to walk to the meeting than wait for a tow truck."

Beth nodded, as if this made sense to her, although it sounded unlikely to Diana. "You came through the burying ground before the meeting too," Beth went on, "but you didn't see anything unusual then? Did you take the same route back?"

"You know there's only one path, unless you walk on the grass. I may have walked around my family's plot, but that's a good way from where ... it happened." She mentally shook herself. Why did she keep lapsing into euphemisms? "Brad's body was not there when I came through," she said firmly. "That was about quarter to eight. I guess that means he died—or was killed, if you like—between eight and nine-thirty."

Beth made a note before she closed her pad, stuffed it back into her purse, and said, "Actually, he'd been dead for at least four hours when you found him. I saw the autopsy report."

Having dropped her bombshell, Beth took pity on Diana and promised to send her a copy of her notes from the autopsy report. But Diana would not let her leave until she'd heard the highlights.

Brad had, the medical examiner determined, died between four and six that afternoon from a blow to the back of the head which caused massive hematoma. Apparently, Beth said, he was hit in the one spot in the back of his ear—she showed Diana, who tried not to flinch, on her own skull—that could result in death even from a not very forceful blow. This fact seemed to fascinate Beth more than any other, and she speculated on it at length.

"But," Diana interrupted, "it said a blow *to* the head, not an accidental fall?"

"Good point." Beth thought for a moment. "As I recall, it said, 'massive skull trauma,' or words to that effect. I remember that there was room on the report form for more than one cause of death, one immediate and any number of secondary ones, but I don't recall if one of those was a fall."

Beth picked her carry-all up from the carpet next to the sofa and slung it over her shoulder. "I'd better just try to get a photocopy. I'll go see Doris, or just slip it in with a batch of meeting minutes if I have to. Bye, Diana."

She breezed out, a writer on a quest for truth, leaving Diana still in a state of shock that persisted through the evening. It was not that she and Alex had not discussed the possibility of murder at length, but that had been like plotting a play or a novel. Not real. An autopsy made it all too real. She was able to fall asleep that night only after making up her mind to share this news with the one person she knew would relish every detail and, in doing so, would take the burden of it off her.

Chapter 13

Jane Wagner's bed-and-breakfast, on a secluded street just off the Green, was identified by a discreet sign on the gate to her front garden. There was an even more extensive back garden, and the house itself was a modest Victorian painted pale yellow with white trim. Jane had once threatened to paint it purple with pink windows and orange moldings and see how Brad Gray liked *them* apples, but she had been persuaded to focus her energies on what she really wanted and not what would put up the backs of people who annoyed her. As a result, she had concentrated on more subtle but equally effective advertising, so that her rooms were always full in season and out. And she could afford the extra help that allowed her to spend more time running the small flower shop in what had once been a sun porch attached to the house.

Diana found her there, repotting some of the plants she sold along with garden tools, vases, and cut flowers. The bell on the screen door tinkled when Diana pushed it open. Jane looked up and smiled.

"Hi," she said. "Come to case out the competition?"

"I'm not planning to go into the gardening business," Diana said, knowing full well what Jane meant. Although their homes were entirely different, they were both in the business of letting strangers sleep in them. Their "competition" had thus far, however, consisted mainly in who could outdo the other in dreaming up inexpensive amenities and "extras" that would draw more business. Jane, who had run Willow

Lane Cottage for ten years, had by far the most experience, so Diana was glad to defer to her.

"How are your bookings so far?" she asked.

"Excellent," Jane said with satisfaction, wiping her hands on a rag and then rinsing them off in a small sink behind the counter. "I'm nearly full through June. The sooner you open up, the sooner I can refer the overflow to you. Do you have a website yet? It's made a huge difference in my advertising while scarcely making a dent in the budget."

Diana smiled, grateful for Jane's generosity. "I hope to open fully by June. You'll certainly be the first to know when I'm ready to let people in—especially since I won't be advertising at all to start, not until all the work is finished."

Jane shook her head. "I wish I could have afforded to get everything just the way I wanted before I opened. I had to open the rooms one at a time just to get the business going. Now there are things I want to do in the older rooms, but I can't lose the business while I do them."

"Close for two weeks and send me the overflow," Diana said.

Jane laughed as she pulled her gardening apron off over her jeans and sweatshirt and loosened the ponytail that had held her straight gray hair off her face.

"The operative word is cooperation, not competition," she said, running a hand through her loosened hair. "I'll steer extra business your way, but don't ask me to *give* you my guests."

"Maybe we can trade," Diana suggested.

"What, the ones you don't like for the ones I don't like?"

"Something like that."

Jane grinned. "Let's discuss it over coffee."

She led Diana into her small kitchen, which was occupied mainly by a king-sized refrigerator, a range, and two microwaves. Over the *swoosh* of running water as she washed the last of the potting soil off her hands, Jane said, "Apropos of your opening, I understand congratulations are in order. As far as the government of Middleford is concerned, you can now operate your business as you see fit."

Diana smiled. It was typical of Jane to put it that way. Like Seth Howell, she had little patience with circumlocutions and was in the habit of calling a spade a spade. "I could scarcely believe it when Seth said I was finished—oh, good heavens! I forgot to pay the fee for that septic permit!"

Jane finished working lotion into her hands and pulled two coffee mugs down from a shelf. "Well, that gives you a good excuse, if you don't milk it for too long, to put off the grand opening."

"What do you mean?"

Jane poured coffee and sat down. "You don't mind my being frank, do you, Diana?"

"Jane, dear, I wouldn't have you any other way."

"Well, you know I'm delighted that you've decided to go into the business, and I know you're as meticulous as any finicky cat I've ever owned, but it has taken longer to get that place open than it should have, even given Brad Gray's delaying tactics. To be honest, I began to wonder if you were ... well, afraid of success."

"I don't understand."

"You're so used to a certain kind of success. You succeeded in being born well, marrying well, doing your part and more for the community and the world— plenty of reincarnated saints wouldn't have done as well. But you've never succeeded by your own toil. To be honest, I wasn't sure you could do it. But I was wrong, and I'm delighted to say so to your face."

"Thank you." Diana didn't know what else to say. This was not an aspect of her dream that she had ever considered, but even as Jane said them, she recognized the truth in her words. She *had* been privileged; she *had* gone along with other people's visions for her life. But what Jane didn't know was that Diana had never chafed at this, because she loved every moment she had experienced.

But Jane also didn't know either the extent of her need to change that life now, to strike out on her own and succeed "by her own toil." She didn't know if she could explain this to Jane; she would just have to demonstrate it by making The Inn on the Green a success.

But Jane was not one to belabor a point she had made, however inflammatory or unexpected on the part of its target. "So," she said, "can I give you some more tips on running your business, or did you come for something else?"

Diana was grateful for her frankness, but a little reluctant to invite any more such candor. "What else would there be?" she waffled.

Jane grinned. "Well, for starters, there's that lovely man you've got stashed in your gatehouse. I don't suppose you'd like to give me a hint as to how you snagged him?"

This was another unexpected diversion, even though the look in Jane's eyes said that she was only teasing. Diana stumbled through an explanation, concluding, "I expect he'll be moving out this week." Really, she told herself, she ought to have expected to attract a share of Middlefordians' curiosity about Alex Gordon if she was rash enough to allow him into her house. Or at least her gatehouse.

"I wouldn't count on his moving any time soon," Jane remarked. Diana resisted the temptation to again ask what she meant. Tackling the real reason she came was beginning to look much easier than it had before Jane followed Beth's unsettling revelation with not one, but two of her own.

But reminded of the autopsy report, she plunged ahead.

"I wondered," she began, "what you thought about Bradford Gray's death."

"How do you mean?" Jane was not at all hesitant about asking for explanations. "If you expect me to say I'm glad he's dead, I'm not. I didn't like Brad, but I wouldn't wish that on anyone at his age. He was only fifty-two or -three."

In for a penny, in for a pound, Diana thought, and said, equally directly, "Beth Hudson told me yesterday that she had a tip that Brad's death might not have been an accident. She'd also seen the autopsy report."

Jane's face lit up in anticipation of a fresh—and very rich—source of local gossip. "You don't say! Tell me all!" She may not have reveled in Brad's death, but it was in the past now, and gossip was eternal.

Diana told, in an abbreviated version, what Beth had reported and a little of her own speculations, then gave Jane a few minutes to digest the information while she rose to reheat their forgotten coffee in one of the microwaves. She hoped that Jane would give her an equally easy opening to insert a question about her own movements Wednesday. Not that Diana suspected her, but she knew Jane wouldn't be offended if she blundered in her questioning. And practice made perfect.

But Jane didn't seem to have thought of the possibility of being a suspect herself. "Well," she said, plopping back down into her chair. "I suppose there's no end of people with motives to do Brad in."

"Like who?" Diana said.

"Oh, come on, Diana, we've both tangled with Brad in one way or another. So has almost everyone else in this town, and some of them may have been a lot more resentful. Unlike you and me, not everyone succeeded in outwitting or outflanking Brad and getting what they wanted in the end."

"You mean, your business with the fire doors," Diana ventured.

"Sure. And yours with the septic tank." She gave Diana an assessing look over her mug. "But in case you're wondering, I regarded that battle as my little victory, so I never wanted to get back at Brad for it. Besides, I was here all Wednesday night. Didn't hear about Brad until Enid Peterson called me Wednesday morning. Enid, as you no doubt know, is even more addicted to gossip than I am, and unlike me, doesn't hesitate to spread it over the telephone wires. Be grateful she hasn't yet learned to send e-mail or texts. Did you know, by the way, that her annoying nephew has been sponging off her again?"

"Howard? Wasn't he in some rehab program in Albany?"

"I guess he graduated—or they kicked him out. I saw him coming out of her house a week or so ago, but needless to say, I didn't speak to him.

"Getting back to Brad, though," she went on, "since you ask, I can think of a couple of people who didn't have any luck with Brad. Andy Goodall, for instance, had a run-in with him when Andy was on the Wetlands Commission. I don't remember the details, but Brad managed to reverse some vote that Andy had worked hard to bring about. I doubt he still holds a grudge, but I think Millie may."

Jane stared into space for a minute, and Diana could sense the gears turning in her memory. She smiled, but didn't interrupt.

"And then there's the Dunbars," Jane went on. "They used to be Brad's neighbors, but he complained so long and loud about their bing cherry trees dropping debris over his side of the fence that they finally cut them down—and then moved elsewhere, which of course was just what Brad wanted in the first place. He bought their house, tore it down, and added the lot to his baronial acreage."

Diana's heart sank. "Oh, dear, this is beginning to sound like an embarrassment of riches so far as suspects go. And we've not even started on the theatricals. Beth tells me even Julia Desmond disliked him."

"No surprise, but remember that taking one's resentment to the point of a lethal attack would involve having an ego almost as big as Brad's. I can't see the Goodalls or even the Dunbars having that kind of self-importance, can you? And Seth Howell is too level-headed to let Brad get his goat, even though Brad grabbed at the halter every chance he got. He probably never realized that being the acknowledged leader of any group he belonged to isn't essential to Seth's ego."

One of Jane's guests walked by the window, and Jane waved. "That's the nicest young man. He came for the weekend, but likes it so much here, he's staying on for as long as I have an empty room. Frankly, I think he's an actor trying to find a way into the festival, but he says not, so I have to take him at his word."

Diana turned to look out the window, but caught only a glimpse of fashionably cut brown hair and a tanned hand on the garden gate.

"What about Ben McIlvey?" she asked, getting back to cases.

"Ah, now there's an interesting case. Brad's been walking all over Ben for years, and Ben's not entirely without ego of his own. But he's more ambitious than he is proud, and I don't think he'd gotten to the point where he'd achieved everything he wanted with Brad's help and was ready to ditch him. In his place, though, I might be looking forward to the day I could bash the guy who made my life miserable for years over the head with a blunt instrument."

"Still, that sounds very speculative. How do you know?"

"Well, I don't, which is why I'm telling you and no one else. I don't know Ben very well, although he's closer to my age than to Brad's and we went to school together. We didn't socialize then, and we don't now."

"Do you remember Brad in school? What was he like?"

"Like a junior version of his adult self—a bully, a pain in the posterior. He was a small kid, which may have something to do with it. I think he was sick as a very young child and was sent to some school in Massachusetts up to the fifth or sixth grade, which is when I met him. He'd gotten his health back by then, but he didn't get to his full height until his senior year in high school. By that time, his abrasive personality was fixed in cement."

There was something about this history that struck Diana as wrong, but she couldn't put a finger on it to ask, so she let Jane talk. That was what she'd come for; she'd sort out the facts later.

"So I guess that puts Ben at the top of the suspect list," Jane said with some relish. "He had motive and presumably means and possibly opportunity, although I suppose we must still eliminate everyone else who had to be at Town Hall for the zoning meeting by the same reckoning."

"I thought we were at least eliminating Seth as a possibility."

"No one is above suspicion." Jane had a large library of mystery novels that she kept on hand for her guests. Diana concluded that she must have read all of them herself. She spoke the language fluently.

"Speaking of suspicions," Diana reminded Jane, "what, if anything, happened at the reception after the funeral that might be indicative of anything?"

"It was disappointing all around," Jane admitted. "Marjorie didn't make an appearance—I suppose she wanted to avoid having to remove her veil—and Ben made himself the center of attention, since no one cared enough to stop him. At least the food was good. I wonder if Phillipa Todd catered it?" she mused, referring to the manager of the Festival Theater's official watering hole, the Terrace Café. All the B&B owners in town coveted Phillipa's breakfast recipes, even to holding meetings to discuss possible ingredients and try them out.

"I tell you what," Jane said, snapping out of her speculations. "I'll give this some more thought and make a list of everyone I can think of who had a reason, compelling or not, to want Brad dead and e-mail it to you. I'd like to ask around a little, if you don't mind, and see what I can find out."

"I certainly don't mind if you ask around," Diana said, secretly delighted.

"Well, I wasn't sure if you were taking this on as a cause of your own."

"As another excuse to put off opening the inn?"

Jane had the grace to look embarrassed, a rare thing for her. "Oh, look, Diana, forget I said that. I'm always shooting off my mouth, you know that."

Diana smiled. "I know, but I love you for it, Jane. Don't stop."

"Well, I can at least direct my speculation elsewhere. Why don't we get together again, maybe with Beth, and divide up the investigative chores? In the meanwhile, I'll just pay a few calls on the other B&B owners, especially the ones who grew up in this town. Let's not discount the Mayberry factor—in a place like this, everyone knows everyone else's business, or thinks they do. 'I saw him there that night' and 'No, he was someplace else, I saw him with my own eyes.' You know what I mean.

"Which reminds me," she went on, "why hasn't Kent Brewster been by here about this? I should think he'd be checking everyone's alibis. Not that I have one, strictly speaking. I was on the phone to a bunch of people Wednesday night, but I guess I could have done that from any phone. It wouldn't be hard to be somewhere other than where you say you are, with the technology these days."

"I don't think Kent puts any store in this theory about Brad's death," Diana conceded.

"He's sure it was an accident? Even though Brad apparently died hours before he was found?"

"How do you know that?" Diana demanded.

Jane grinned. "Beth told me. I lure her here with my latest muffin experiments, and she tells me all the juiciest news."

"I might have known," Diana conceded. "The autopsy report does seem to indicate that it was an accident—or at any rate, it didn't mention homicide—and Kent says that what the medical examiner decrees is good enough for him. Anyway, you know he was friends with Brad, so I expect he would just as soon put the whole thing behind him."

"As much of a friend as Brad ever had, I suppose," Jane said, staring thoughtfully out the window.

"What do you mean?"

Jane looked at her intently, as if considering what to reveal. Then she shrugged, apparently concluding that anything she said couldn't hurt anyone now.

"This was before your time—and mine too, for that matter—but Brad and Kent and Larraine were in high school together. Brad dated Larraine, but she turned his marriage proposal down in favor of Kent's. She was always a smart girl, and I guess she knew that Kent was a better bet in the long run. Brad's always resented that."

"But that was so long ago," Diana objected.

"True, but I wonder if there wasn't something more recent to strain the relationship. Maybe Brad lent Kent money—or the other way around, even, since Brad was always into some risky financial speculation, if only to keep Marjorie in her Guccis." She paused, having broken even more fertile ground for speculation.

"They say," she added, "that most murders are committed by a spouse or family member."

"I believe that's the theory," Diana said, "but I don't see Marjorie caring enough to get that angry. Or succumbing to any strong passion, but admittedly I don't know her all that well."

"I do," Jane said. "I knew her when she was still Marjorie Bonning. She was only two years ahead of me in school—which she'd never admit." She laughed and fingered her gray hair. "Maybe if I dyed my hair and had cosmetic surgery, she'd be more willing to be seen with me. Except for grown kids, there's nothing that will make you look older than a schoolmate with gray hair and laugh lines."

"Maybe she's vain," Diana conceded. "But capable of murder?"

"I'd guess most self-centered people are capable of murder, if their sense of self gets enough of a shock.

What's *her* alibi for Wednesday night—or afternoon, as the case may be?"

"I don't know. As you said at the funeral, she must have been home hiding her facelift."

"That doesn't make her physically housebound," Jane said, then added with relish, "She could have gone out incognito—or is it incognita? Anyway, I've seen her wig collection."

"Jane ..."

"Hmm?"

"Do you think you could find out where Marjorie was?"

Jane sat back and gaped at Diana, who wasn't sure if her friend was appalled or delighted. "Why, Diana Quick! You're turning into a regular Miss Marple. Was all this your idea, or have you been discussing it with D.C. Dickson?"

Diana felt herself redden. "Well, I have, actually. But now—well, I guess I just can't dismiss the idea, even if it isn't any of my business."

"That's the best way to look at it," Jane confirmed. "If you really had a stake in it, you couldn't be objective. It's like gossip—it's only harmful if you have a personal vendetta against someone."

That sounded very much like Alex Gordon's advice. "But—"

"What?"

"If we turn out to be right, someone *will* be hurt."

Jane leaned forward and grasped Diana's hand. "Someone already has been, remember? We're not out to get someone here, just to find out the truth."

"But the one leads to the other."

"Possibly. But we can't just let it go now."

"*We?*"

Jane grinned. "You don't think you can leave me out now, do you? What's our next move, Miss M?"

Chapter 14

Over the next few days, Diana attacked the work still needing to be done at the inn with renewed vigor, keeping Jane's unsettling observation about her "fear of success" in the back of her mind. *This is not a hobby*, she reminded herself. *I am not a dilettante.* The inn would open this summer, and it would succeed. This was now a fact, a predetermined conclusion, in Diana's mind. Or so she continued to assure herself.

Nonetheless, her conversation with Jane about the plethora of suspects in Bradford Gray's murder—if indeed it was a murder, she reminded herself—kept rising to the top of her mind, along with a restlessness to continue what she had begun with Alex Gordon's provocative prodding.

Alex had been notably missing since he set her on this quest, which was annoying of him in the extreme. Not that she wanted his help, or needed it, she told herself, but all this was really his idea and it was too bad of him to abandon it. It was true that he had not actually moved out, his belongings evidence that he at least slept in the gatehouse, and it was equally true that the opening of *Romeo and Juliet* was only two weeks away—Mark Edwards having declared an extra two weeks at the start and end of each year's season for preparation of both the coming season and, in September, the next summer's. Alex had his job to do, the one he mocked so lightly, but which obviously meant a great deal to him.

Still, she wished they could talk again. True to her word, Beth Hudson had faxed a copy of her notes of the autopsy report to Diana, although she did wonder why she could not simply make a copy of the document itself. She would have liked to show that to Alex, if only to brag about her initiative in obtaining it and to point out that it contained the word 'probable' before 'accident' as the cause of death. But she also needed his perspective, a perspective that Jane, in her eagerness to dig up dirt, lacked. She needed to ask him what she—they—should do next.

Diana was scrubbing out her pantry when her next move came to her under its own power. She needed to stop adding names to her list of suspects in Brad Gray's death and start eliminating some. The least likely should be the easiest, but her imagination balked at asking Andrew Goodall or Irene Dunbar where they were from four to six Wednesday afternoon. She straightened up and said to Margo Black, her housekeeper, that she had just remembered an errand she had to run.

"Would you mind finishing this?" she said, handing Margo the bucket.

"I offered to do it in the first place," Margo said reproachfully, yanking the bucket out of Diana's hand and sloshing soapy water over the floor she had just wiped clean. "Why you've suddenly come down with a yen to do manual labor is beyond me."

Margo had been helping Diana put the inn to rights since she first had the idea, and they had established a comfortable working relationship despite Margo's tendency to grumble and Diana's to start projects she forgot to finish—which, in light of her new determination to succeed, she should overcome. But not today. Today Margo would be on her own, and although Diana hated to think more work would get done that way, she was eager to put her idea into action.

"I know I can't do it better than you can," she said, "but frankly, sometimes I just need the manual work to occupy my hands so my brain can think."

Margo relaxed her expression. "I know what you mean. I've worked out all kinds of problems at the ironing board or when I've had my hands submerged in soapy water. Okay, get along to wherever you're going. If I'm not here when you get back, I'll be by same time tomorrow unless I hear differently from you. Don't forget that you were going to move the paintings off the stairwell walls so that I can clean up there."

"I won't forget. Thanks," Diana said gratefully.

She ran upstairs to change out of her paint-stained jeans and T-shirt into something appropriate for a firmly established Middleford resident out to pass a neighborly afternoon with similarly situated citizens.

She made Town Hall her first destination, where she hoped town clerk Doris Mallory might fill in at least a few missing pieces of information. Doris greeted her with a reminder that she had not yet paid the fee for her septic permit.

"Yes, that's why I've come," Diana said mendaciously. "I'm afraid it completely slipped my mind."

"I thought it might have," Doris remarked as she pulled documents out of a tray and Diana fished for her checkbook. "I mean, with finding Brad that night and all, I can understand how some details could slip your mind...." Doris fixed her round blue eyes hopefully on Diana, who could not have conjured up a better opening for her queries.

Diana smiled at Doris, grateful for her avid curiosity, and as she wrote out a check and signed the forms

Doris gave her, she wondered how far she could question the town clerk without arousing suspicion instead of her normal inquisitiveness. Well, as Jane might have said, there was only one way to find out.

"It *was* rather upsetting," she confided. "I'd wondered, like everyone else, I guess, why Brad wasn't at the meeting, but I wasn't thinking about him at all by the time I left." She glanced at Doris, who had rolled her desk chair forward and was listening with interest, her mouth slightly open and her ears practically humming. Thus encouraged, Diana went on, "Did you hear from him at all—I mean, to say that he might not be able to get to the meeting, or that he'd be late?"

Doris shook her head. "He didn't call, and he hadn't been here all day, though that's not unusual, since he's got a business to run. I figured he'd show up for the meeting as usual, so I didn't worry about it."

"Were you here the whole day?"

"Nine to five, like a good little trooper. I went over to the Colonial Café for supper then and got back about six. I had some files to pull for the meeting. There was no one else here yet when I got back to the office."

Diana made a mental note to check the café, then asked, hoping a general question would yield some specific answers, "When do people generally start coming in, when there's a meeting? Do you lock up when you go out to dinner? Does anyone else have a key?"

Doris didn't seem to find so many questions suspicious. "Most people don't get here until the last minute," she said. "That night, though, Seth got here at about quarter past seven. He said he needed to look something up and I let him into the deed vault. He has a key to the front door, but I'm the only one who can access anything that's locked up inside. Jesse and Ben got in about ten minutes before eight—just before everyone with business before the board started coming in. Of course, there was that delay before they could actually start the meeting, but everyone who had to be here—except you, I guess—was here by five past."

"Did you see Ben McIlvey during the day?"

Doris shook her head. "It was a pretty quiet day. No one came in except, I think, a lady looking for a dog license and two people wanting yard sale permits. Beth Hudson was here for a while, too, in the morning, reading old minutes. I made some copies for her, which as I recall were from earlier meetings when some of the same agenda items came up."

Diana thanked her, picked up her permit, and left the building. She paused briefly on the steps, to write the times Doris had mentioned in a notebook she'd brought for the purpose and stashed in her shoulder bag. She sighed. Doris's information was a start, but not a lot of help if Brad died as early as four or five o'clock. She'd still have to check out everyone's whereabouts earlier in the day. It looked more and more as if she'd have to take Jane up on her eager offer of help.

Most of the offices in Town Hall were on a lower level than the public meeting rooms, and as Diana climbed back to street level, she glanced around with new eyes. Everything looked so normal. In the center of what was usually called "The Alley," a wide street where traffic was no longer allowed so that people with town business as well as the patrons of the businesses across the way could walk safely, was a small garden. That hadn't been Brad Gray's idea, oddly enough. Funds for it had been raised by contributions from town residents and an assortment of charitable fund-raisers. It did look nice, Diana thought, crossing it and stopping to read the inscription on the monument to a former town librarian.

Since it was lunchtime, she made her way to the Colonial Café, one of the businesses on the other side of The Alley, and ordered a chicken salad sandwich. A chat with the waitress yielded the information that Doris Mallory had dinner there before every town meeting, to save her the long ride home and back; Doris lived outside the town center, on a remote country lane.

That eliminated Doris as a suspect, Diana supposed. Although the town clerk had never been on her list, it gave her at least a small feeling of satisfaction. She glanced around the café wondering if anyone actually on her list might be there. In its very small way, the Colonial Café was like Paris, where it was said that if you sat at a sidewalk café long enough, someone you knew from home would stroll by. In Middleford, everyone—with the possible exception of Marjorie Gray—ate at the Colonial Café at least occasionally.

Then, as if to prove this true by sheer force of Diana's wishful thinking, Rebecca Fox appeared next to her booth.

"Hi, Diana. May I join you?"

"Sure," Diana said. Rebecca had been a schoolmate of Diana's before Diana's parents sent her to a boarding school in the next county. More to the present point, Rebecca was Irene Dunbar's daughter and had the same pale, freckled complexion and big green eyes. Maybe she had the same grudge against Brad Gray too, or at least her parents' dislike of the man.

"That looks good," Rebecca said, eying Diana's sandwich. She ordered one, and then, while Diana was contemplating how to open the subject of Brad's death, she had another stroke of luck.

"There's Millie Goodall," said Rebecca, who was facing the door. "Millie! Join us!" She glanced at Diana apologetically then, realizing her gaffe. "Oh, Diana, I'm sorry—do you mind?"

"No, of course not," Diana assured her sincerely, as Mildred Goodall greeted them both and slid into the booth next to Rebecca. Mildred had been Diana and Rebecca's fourth-grade teacher, and while Diana could still name all her grade-school teachers, Miss Charles, as she was then, was one of her favorites. Mildred had married Andrew Goodall when she was fifty and promptly retired from teaching, but she kept in touch with her old pupils.

"How are you girls?" she said and, almost in the same breath, told the waitress, "The soup-and-salad special, dressing on the side." Then she turned to Diana. "My dear, I'm so sorry—that you had to be the one to find Brad, I mean."

Diana had some difficulty hiding her delight at this easy opening, so she lowered her eyes. "It was a shock, of course, but I've been so busy with the inn, I've not really had time to think about it." That was an outright fib, and she wondered if lying was coming too easily to her. "I saw you at the funeral, Millie, but I didn't want to trouble you . . ."

Millie shook her head sadly. "I know. Andy told me I was making a spectacle of myself, weeping like that. But I'd just then realized that this was the first funeral of one of my students I'd ever attended—well, except for poor Billy Peck's years ago, when he was killed in that stupid hunting accident. I always thought that you all should outlive me by decades. Life just isn't fair, is it?"

Diana thought about all the people who had disliked Brad, possibly even enough to kill him, and marveled at Millie's good-heartedness. She had more than likely never thought negatively even of Brad. Better still, the mystery of why she had been crying at his funeral was solved. She smiled and patted Millie's hand.

"I walked by your place a few days ago," Millie said, tactfully changing the subject, "and couldn't help noticing how nice it looked. That dark green trim is very attractive with the white."

Diana thanked her and gave both ladies an update of her activities with the inn, then asked Millie, "Was that Wednesday you walked by? I don't recall seeing you at the Zoning Commission meeting."

The question sounded very contrived to Diana's ears, but she had decided that eliminating suspects by motive would take forever, and she would have to revert to elimination by lack of opportunity. It would likely be easier anyway to find out where people were during the "window of opportunity," as she had heard it called. Checking out their alibis, as Jane would say.

"No, that was Sunday, after church," Millie said, apparently not hearing anything unusual in Diana's question. "On Wednesday, Andy and I were in Bennington visiting Andy's granddaughter. She's finishing college there this year, you know."

The problem with chatting with people one had known all one's life, Diana realized, was that one was obliged to listen with a show of interest to all the family news since the last meeting with the old friend in question. Fortunately, Millie was not verbose, and it was not long before she recalled the original question. Diana remembered now that Miss Charles had had a disconcerting way of remembering a student's earlier mistakes just when the student had thought them forgotten. Now, however, this worked to Diana's advantage.

"Andy and I rarely attend town government meetings anymore," she said. "And I suppose I needn't tell you why. Naturally, I'm always happy to see a former student of mine succeed, but ..."

"Brad was your student? In fourth grade?"

"No, it happened that I was teaching sixth grade that year. I went back to fourth the year after—I liked teaching the younger ones—so that was the last I saw of Brad as his teacher. As you know, the grade school combined some grades at that time because there were so few students locally. It was just before you came, Diana, that the school population grew large enough that all the grades could have their own classrooms and teachers."

She smiled at Rebecca. "And of course, Rebecca's little ones are too young to have had the privilege of my tutoring."

"And sorry I am they've had to miss it," Rebecca assured her.

Diana had long since finished her sandwich and so, finding no good reason to stay, and no other "suspects" having entered the cafe, she said good-bye and left. As she was walking back into the center of town, however, she met Jesse Connolly's wife Eleanor on the street. Eleanor was, fortunately, voluble on the subject of Brad Gray, and let drop the information that she and Jesse had had dinner out that day with George and Irene Dunbar, Rebecca's parents, at the Lakeside Inn before George left to attend the meeting. This brought the names scratched off Diana's list to three. She reminded herself that she ought to check this "alibi" with the inn, but reasoned that there was no urgency to do so.

She smiled. So far this "investigation" reminded her of one of the scavenger hunts Irene had always organized for Rebecca's childhood birthday parties. One find led so easily to another that Diana had the sensation—which she knew, even at that age, could as easily dissipate with her next step—of reaching the prize with no effort at all.

She looked at her list again. Three crossed-off names seemed a drop in a very large bucket.

And it had been almost a week since Brad's death. People's memories would be fading. She should persevere if she was going to finish this—and get back to her life as it had been before last Wednesday. Again, Jane's impression of her as reluctant to blaze a trail of her own prodded her on.

Diana walked home by way of the Green and sat down on one of the wooden seats attached to the bandstand in the middle to think. Who else was at the meeting that night? She cursed herself for not getting a copy of the minutes while she was in Town Hall and was debating retracing her steps when she remembered three names.

Ben McIlvey.

Marjorie Gray.

Mark Edwards.

She thought about the third name for a while, as surely the easiest to eliminate. But she could come up with no earthly reason to question Mark, with whom she had only a passing acquaintance, about his activities a week before. On the other hand, Nigel had invited her to drop by to watch a rehearsal of *Romeo and Juliet* whenever she liked, and she had yet to do so. She glanced at her watch. Rehearsals started at one, he'd told her, and went on indefinitely. She had plenty of time to go to the theater, so she contemplated Marjorie Gray and Ben McIlvey for a moment.

Perhaps she shouldn't have given Jane the task of looking into Marjorie's whereabouts Wednesday afternoon. Not that she didn't trust Jane, but she would have liked to see Marjorie herself, to look into her face for the kind of thing no plastic surgeon could alter— character. Was Marjorie Gray capable of killing her husband, or did she not care enough to take that kind of desperate action?

Diana sighed. She was speculating again on motivations she couldn't prove. Better to stick to proving or disproving alibis. She turned her mind to Ben McIlvey.

Ben and Brad's real estate office was at the north end of town, within easy distance of several of the new developments they had pioneered, and might well close at five, unlike the theater.

"Nothing ventured, nothing gained," she reminded herself and decided to confront the prime suspect in his den while she still had the confidence to do so. She knew well enough that her confidence faded quickly in the light of even the mildest setback. She recalled her mother taking her to a musical play when she was a child, an operetta whose name she'd forgotten. It had been magical for a six-year-old, until one point in the second act. As an introduction to a song about love, the tenor had been teasing his lady-love about "three little words" he wanted to say to her. "Can you guess what they are?" he asked the soprano, upon which Diana had piped up from the audience, "I love you! That's right, Mama, isn't it?" The rest of the audience had laughed delightedly, but Diana had heard only her mother's whispered "Hush!" and seen her embarrassed look, as if she would have liked to give her daughter away then and there to any of these laughing fools who'd take her.

Since then, and until Daniel—and even with him, to some extent—Diana had kept her emotions very close to her heart.

She shook her head to rid her mind of useless memories and stood up. Ben's office. She'd get her car and go there—and think of something to say on the way.

Chapter 15

Diana didn't have to use the rather lame excuse she invented, about leaving some advertising flyers for the Inn on the Green, to call in Ben's real estate office. As soon as she walked in the door, he spotted her and intercepted her before she was halfway to his secretary's desk. He didn't even question her sudden appearance when she'd never been to his office before.

"Diana! Just the person I was trying to reach. Thanks for coming by."

"Ben ... of course. No trouble. What is it you wanted?"

"Come into my office. Can I get you something? Cup of coffee?"

He escorted her into a large, thickly carpeted office, which struck Diana as pretty luxurious for a junior partner—until she realized that it must have been Brad's office. Ben certainly hadn't wasted any time taking over.

"Nothing for me, thanks." Diana glanced around, looking for some evidence of Brad's recent presence. His name was on most of the plaques and awards decorating one wall, but decided they were still there simply to impress. Ben's name was on only a few of them.

She sat down where he indicated, in a plush red-leather easy chair that seemed to swallow her up. Still trying to sort out this unexpected welcome, Diana found her imagination jumping through irrelevant hoops. Perhaps the chair had been in Ben's old office;

he was a big man, and the chair was just the right size for him, like Papa Bear's in the Little Red Riding Hood story. She looked around for a bowl of porridge. Instead, she met Ben's assessing gaze.

Was she mistaken in the avarice she saw in his eyes?

"I'll get right to the point, Diana," Ben said, leaning back in his own chair. It creaked under his weight. "I was driving by the lake the other day and remembered your bungalow up there. I stopped by—didn't think you'd mind, I didn't go in or anything. Thing is— would you be willing to sell it?"

"Sell the cottage?" This was unexpected. The lakeside property, an hour's drive north of Middleford, at the farthest end of Mirror Lake, had been Daniel's favorite retreat, and had belonged to his family, not hers. She had liked spending time there with him, but had used it with decreasing frequency in recent years.

She was not surprised that Ben was aware of this. He was watching her closely to gauge her reaction. "I know you don't get as much use out of it as you once did," he went on, "and you're tied up with the inn now, getting ready to open and all. I'm not asking for a listing, Diana. It's for me. I like the place and I'd keep it up. Wouldn't change a thing. And I'd give you a fair price."

"Well, I don't know, Ben. I hadn't thought of selling it."

"You don't have to give me an answer now, Diana. I just wanted to mention it, give you a chance to think it over. Of course, it would be great if I could have it soon, use it this summer. You know."

"Of course." She rose to leave, and he didn't try to stop her, getting up to open the door. "I'll think about it, Ben. I'll let you know soon. It's just that ... well, this is an unexpected offer."

"I believe in striking while the iron is hot, you know. Or maybe that's the wrong phrase. I guess I mean I'm acting on an impulse."

He laughed at his own clumsiness with language, and despite her efforts to subtly remove his arm from her shoulder, he walked her out to her car.

"You know, Diana," he said confidentially, when they were out of earshot of anyone in the office, "I wanted to say, I'm sorry you had to be the one to ... you know, find Brad's body. It must have been tough."

"Yes. Thanks." She suddenly didn't want to discuss it with him.

"It was almost me, you know. I'd walked through the burying ground myself that afternoon, maybe about six o'clock, on my way to Town Hall. I needed to look up some property records. Thought I'd get it done when I had to be there anyway— you know, for the meeting. But Kent told me later that Brad couldn't have been there before eight, or you'd have seen him on your way to the meeting. Is that right?"

"Yes, that's right. Well, thanks, Ben. I'll certainly think over your offer."

"That's all I ask, Diana. All I ask."

He closed the car door when she'd gotten in and waved as she drove off, so unsteady at the wheel that she pulled over as soon as she was out of Ben's sight, took a deep breath, and thought about that bizarre conversation.

Had Ben just deliberately given her an alibi for himself for the time of Brad's death? The times he gave her were wrong, but he might well not know about the autopsy findings that Beth had revealed to her and Jane.

And Doris Mallory said he hadn't been at Town Hall that afternoon until almost eight.

Why was Ben McIlvey lying to her?

Chapter 16

The Festival Theater was at the end of Main Street, before it turned into the state highway at the town line. The theater, referred to as the Mainstage to distinguish it from the Music Faire, was a barnlike wooden building that nonetheless had a cozy feel to it and, being well insulated and thoroughly air conditioned, was comfortable in the summer and usable by local civic groups in the winter. As a teenager, Diana had worked backstage and in the office for both the festival and an annual variety show put on by the Community Club.

Nigel had told her rehearsals began at one o'clock, and they were apparently well under way when she walked through the lobby and cautiously pushed open one side of the double doors to the auditorium. About halfway down the rows of seats, five people sat with their heads together, while on stage a young man in jeans and a paint-stained sweatshirt was directing several other young people who were moving furniture. The house lights were on, but the back rows of seats were in semi-darkness. Diana slipped into an aisle seat and waited to get her bearings.

She studied the backs of the heads of the people a dozen rows down from her and spotted Mark Edwards's curly, slightly graying hair in the middle of Row M. She spent a futile five minutes trying to think of some acceptable way to approach him and open a conversation that might reasonably lead to answers to her questions about his whereabouts Wednesday afternoon. While she was pondering this, the young man on the stage cleared everyone off it, and the lights in the ceiling of the theater came on and illuminated the set.

Immediately, the flat, wooden structure took on a golden glow, like mellowed marble. The flimsy fake buildings around the edge of the stage solidified, and the floor turned into a paved square. Behind empty windows lamplight glowed, and the faint hum of sewing machines backstage turned to lute music.

A throng of half-costumed actors entered and began milling about. Fascinated, Diana watched Verona come to life as two servants detached themselves from the crowd and began a discussion of the feud between the Montagues and Capulets, followed rapidly by two representatives of the two opposing families, whose interchange was interrupted abruptly by a shout from the auditorium. Diana jumped.

"Abraham and Balthasar!" Mark Edwards called out. "Take it faster! Balthasar, quit fiddling with your sword! Again, from the beginning."

The first set of actors scrambled back into position, and this time the scene went much more quickly. Tybalt came on, uninterrupted by instructions from the auditorium, then the Capulets. The noise on stage escalated to the point that Diana guessed Mark might not have been heard had he chosen to interrupt again.

Then a sudden hush fell, and heads turned toward center stage. Alex Gordon stood there, arms akimbo, glaring at the assembled crowd, every inch the Prince despite the jeans and T-shirt he wore. It was as if he had been in darkness and light had just been turned on him, although Diana was certain that the lighting had not changed. He took a few steps forward as he began his speech, admonishing his subjects to cease their quarreling. By the time he reached his last line—"Once more, on pain of death, all men depart"—he had taken full control of the stage, and as he exited, followed by a coterie of servants, there was a momentary silence before Montague remembered his next line.

Before he could utter it, Mark Edwards said into the stillness, "I think you've got it, Alex." There was a half-amused, half-exasperated note in his voice. Alex stepped out of stage right and said, "But you want to hear it again?"

"No, thanks. I've think you've put the fear of God into them."

Alex turned to the assembled cast and made the sign of the cross over them, like the pope blessing the masses, which gesture, oddly enough, made them break into laughter. Mark let it go on for a few seconds before signaling the stage manager to call a halt.

"All right, everyone," said the SM, a tall, thin woman with a deep voice that poorly matched her physique, "Places please. From 'Who set this ancient quarrel'."

The rehearsal went on, but Diana heard none of it. Instead she sat pondering the mysteries of stage presence, which led her to wondering how some people were able to control everyone around them without seeming to exert any control. Daniel had been able to do that, too, and he was no actor. Diana, on the other hand, had never been able to do it. Perhaps it was solely a masculine power—or at least a masculine attribute, for she had known other women who had it. One had to admire it, but it was not always easy to live with.

Daniel had convinced her that he would not have been as successful as he had been in his career without her support, and she had accepted that as a compliment. It gave her a purpose, even if later in their marriage she had begun to wonder if it had been a tactful fabrication.

If she allowed herself to become involved with Alex Gordon....

No, she was already involved, whether she'd intended it or not. She was certainly attracted to him, and she knew instinctively that he would respond to any overture she made. But she was far from certain that she wanted another supporting role at the side of yet another great man—even, while she shared this murder investigation with him, as a second-fiddle Dr. Watson to his symphony-conductor Sherlock.

She had come home to start her own life at last; she did not want to postpone that again even for such a comfortable life as she'd had with Daniel. Somehow, she would have to convey this to Alex, to prevent his making the overture she dared not make herself.

She was startled out of her reverie just then by the sound of someone sliding into the seat beside her.

"Penny for your thoughts," Alex said.

Apparently she had been so lost in those thoughts that he had to enter the row of seats from the far end to attract her attention. She shrugged. "Don't waste your penny."

"How long have you been here?"

"Not long. Since that last scene started."

"Then you haven't missed anything. There was just a lot of boring blocking before that, although I think Mark wants to get through Act One as quickly as possible this morning."

"It doesn't seem to be moving along very fast. Opening night isn't far off."

"Don't remind me. But it's better than it looks. Everyone's off the book—I mean, they've all learned their lines—so it's mainly a matter of tempo now, smoothing out the bumps and glitches."

When she was silent for a moment, he said, "You didn't come here just to watch me posturing, did you?"

She thought he sounded hopeful that she'd come just to see him, and for a moment she was tempted to tell him she had. It wasn't the least reason she'd come.

"Well, no," she admitted. "As a matter of fact, I didn't know you'd be here. You said it was a bit part."

"You needn't be quite that candid," he said, acting affronted. "It *is* a bit part—just that speech and another at the end. 'Not much meat on her, but what's there is cherce.' "

She smiled. "All right, I'll admit I was impressed."

"That's my girl. But getting back to your reason for coming here ... are you by any chance doing some sleuthing?"

"I'd intended to," she said, "but I can't think how to go about what I came for."

"Which is?"

"Questioning Mark Edwards."

When he frowned, she added, "We *did* put him on our list of suspects, remember? I just thought it might be best to eliminate the least likely ones once and for all. At least, so far as their alibis go."

She turned slightly in her seat to see his expression. "I've decided that you're right," she conceded, "about concentrating on opportunity."

She thought that had placated him somewhat. "All right," he said. "What do you need to know?"

"Where he was between four o'clock last Wednesday and the time he arrived at Town Hall for the meeting."

"I'll find out. It will be easier for me anyway."

She was grateful for that, and told him so. Despite her misgivings, it was just common sense to let him do what was easier for him than for her. Besides, she had a triumph of her own to tell him about.

"But confirming Mark's whereabouts is just for form's sake now. Ben McIlvey's moved to the top of the list."

She told him about her morning rounds of the town clerk's office and the Colonial Café, concluding triumphantly with her meeting with Ben McIlvey and his apparently blatant lie about his whereabouts on the afternoon in question. Alex was gratifyingly stunned into momentary silence.

Then he said, "He must have heard you were looking into the so-called accident and thought he could throw you off by being candid. But the man's an idiot. Even if he didn't know that you'd already checked with Town Hall, did he think you wouldn't check his story? Oh, blast!"

"What?"

"I wonder if your Chief Brewster took casts of the footprints in the graveyard. It was muddy enough to show plenty, but by now they'll have been trampled over."

"Oh, you mean that would have placed Ben there— or not. His feet are probably as big as the rest of him. They'd have been easy to spot."

Her regretful tone made him smile. "Still, we can check him out some other way. What else have you been up to today?"

"Is anyone on our list working here—backstage, I mean? Local residents quite often do fill in on non-Equity jobs."

"I've noticed that. As a matter of fact, one of our lighting crew, who oddly enough *is* an Equity member, is also on your zoning board. Bill Burnell. I think he was here on the afternoon in question, however."

"I didn't know Bill knew anything about lighting."

"You may find out all sorts of things you didn't know, hanging about here."

"And some I wish I didn't?"

"You said it, I didn't. Come on, I'll give you a backstage tour. They won't need me for the rest of the act."

"Aren't you meant to provide an inspiring presence?"

"Sometimes I think the sentiments I inspire aren't quite what I'd like to provoke."

She gave him a sharp glance, but he didn't seem to realize how closely he'd touched on her own earlier thoughts about roles that had been chosen for her, and those she'd imposed on herself.

He gave her his hand to help her up, then guided her up the aisle and around the back of the last row of the auditorium to a door into the area open during performances for audience members to reach the lobby and bar. He turned away from the lobby, though, and opened a second door; this came out on a short staircase that led up to the backstage area. By now Diana could scarcely remember where she was in relation to the outside world.

A number of people were standing around in the semidarkness watching the stage, where Act One was now in full swing, moving at an accelerated assembly-line rate, as if everyone wanted to get it over with. Diana guessed that the director used this method to get the actors used to a quickened pace and congratulated herself at her growing theatrical savvy.

As they passed the light board, Diana saw Bill Burnell and whispered to Alex to stop, but the stage manager, clipboard in hand, turned her head and frowned at them, like a stern schoolmistress about to rebuke a disruptive pupil. Alex smiled apologetically at her. Diana was amused to see that she didn't smile back, but just turned again to the action on stage.

"Obsequiousness gets you nowhere with SM's," he whispered when they had reached the far backstage and put another door between them and the rehearsal. Diana looked around, and it struck her that she had not been in this part of the theater since it was in the building stages; Daniel had accompanied her then—or rather, she had tagged along when Daniel invited her parents to tour his new pride and joy. She had been home from boarding school on her summer break before leaving for college, a time when her future had seemed particularly cloudy. She hadn't yet seen Daniel in it.

"Diana?"

"What?"

He was watching her, an amused smile on his lips. "You were miles away."

"Years," she said. "I was remembering the first time I saw the inside of the theater—except that a lot of it was still exposed to the elements at the time. The roof was only half-finished. ..."

He looked as if he wanted to ask for details, but he said only, "How is it we never met before?"

She knew what he meant, but wasn't eager to go into where she had been when he had his first season at Middleford. Not here, at any rate, and not just now. She smiled and said, "I guess Fate was against us."

"Oh, no." He smiled. "I think Fate has just been waiting for us to catch up with each other."

This time, she didn't have to ask what he meant. He seemed to be waiting for a response, but she said nothing, and just then Benvolio brushed past them, calling a greeting to Alex as he divested himself of the outer layers of his costume. He would have stopped, but he was followed closely by a noisy, laughing crowd of actors hurrying off stage. The act was over.

Chapter 17

"Lunch break," Alex said as he slipped past her, lightly touching her arm as he went. "I'll go find Mark now, before he comes in to give notes."

Then he was gone. "Lunch?" Diana asked herself. She glanced at her watch; it was half past four.

"Mistress Quickly!" Nigel's delighted voice came from behind her. "What brings you here?"

"I think I took a wrong turn at Town Hall," she said, aware that her reason didn't matter. The atmosphere had already taken on the coming-down-from-a-high tone she was familiar with from after-hours parties at the inn.

Nigel laughed. "Lucky us that you did. Have a drink." He took her elbow and steered her to an assortment of chairs on the other side of what appeared to be a rehearsal space. Opposite was a raised platform on which two actors were miming bowing to each other.

"I'm confused," she said. "I thought this was a lunch break."

"It is, but I refer to assorted colas, fruit juices, and non-lethal potions. No alcohol permitted until after dinner break, which I should mention won't be before ten o'clock, so you needn't wait up for us."

"Don't worry, I won't. And I'll have a mineral water, if there is one."

Nigel laughed and gave her a quick hug before leaving her in front of an elegant winged chair, which had been vacated an instant before by Bernardo. She was generally grateful for her charges' care for her comforts, but occasionally she wished they would treat her less like a den mother and more like one of them. Or at least closer to their ages. She sat down, feeling every bit of forty-something.

Prince Paris pulled up a chair next to hers; it was a moment before Diana recognized him as the same young man who had stayed at the inn two seasons before, the year she began taking in actors. He'd been a gangly nineteen-year-old then, but had since gained both muscle and maturity—and cut his hair so that his striking facial bones were more prominent. He'd learned a lot about image, she thought. He asked how the renovations were coming, and she filled him in, while the general chaos around them diminished somewhat and people paired up, drifted off, or approached her in some curiosity.

"You're Diana Quick, aren't you?" asked Lady Capulet. She had taken off her headdress, and Diana saw that she was much younger and prettier than she looked on stage as Juliet's mother. Of course, Diana supposed, in medieval Verona, Juliet's mother would have been young by twenty-first-century standards. So, for that matter, would have been Mistress Quickly, her namesake in *Merry Wives*. She hadn't considered that and perked up briefly.

"My name is Nora Peale," the girl said. "I think you know a friend of mine—Jim Bishop?"

"Yes, of course," Diana said. She smiled and invited Nora to sit down in the chair Paris had politely vacated. "Jim has been planting some lovely landscaping for me. I hope that's not taking him away from his work here."

"Oh, no," Nora said. "He's rehearsing *Pericles,* but that's not on deck until July. I told him he should have taken a musical part in the meanwhile."

Diana remembered that Jim had started out in musical theater and was now trying to make a name for himself in the Mainstage program, fighting the Montague and Capulet-like dichotomy between the two disciplines that decreed each should stay on its own turf. She wondered if the real attraction for him here was Nora.

"What brings *you* here?" Nora asked. Diana wondered how many more times she'd hear that question.

"She came for the waters," Nigel said, reappearing just then and handing Diana a bottle of Eau Canada and a plastic glass.

"What waters?" Nora obliged. "We're in the desert."

"I was misinformed," Diana put in, to keep the game going. Nora laughed; Nigel looked pained. Molly, the Irish setter Diana had thought belonged to Jim Bishop, crept out from under a bench, and Nora gave the dog a biscuit from a baggie she carried in her pocket. So Molly belonged to Nora. Diana smiled, confirmed in her conviction that Nora and Jim would soon be a source of gossip, if they weren't already.

"That dog should have a part," Paris said.

"She's Irish," Nigel objected, "not Italian."

"At least she's not a Sassenach like you," Bernardo said, joining them. Diana noticed that he still spoke in the slight Italian accent he used on stage and wondered if it was real. Nigel looked as if he was about to launch into a spirited defense of his nationality, thought better of it and, gathering his dignity around him with his cloak, excused himself.

"I'll have my lunch outside," he muttered, "where the air is fresher." He gave Diana a look that asked her to join him, but she shook her head, then smiled to soften the rejection.

No one objected to Nigel's leaving, and an instant later, their attention focused on Diana again as Nora asked, "Is it true there's been murder done in dear old staid Middleford?"

"Good heavens!" Diana exclaimed. "Who told you that?" She wasn't sure if she should respond first to the rumor of foul deeds or the possible disparagement of her hometown. She decided that Nora had meant "staid" in a friendly way, and in any case it was more important to downplay the idea of murder.

"If you mean Brad Gray, the police are satisfied it was an accident," she said cautiously. It might be interesting to get some outsiders' opinions, even if Nora meant the question only as a tease. "Have you heard differently?"

"You'll have to forgive us," Paris said. "We tend to speculate on a total lack of facts."

"Not total," Nora said. "We know the victim died from a blow on the head. That part was in the *Weekly Citizen*."

"An accidental blow," Diana amended.

"Says who?" Bernardo asked, and when Paris scoffed, he added. "No one saw him fall, did they?"

"No, but—"

"Have the police investigated everyone's alibi?" Bernardo asked Diana.

"I don't think so," she said, trying to look interested but indifferent at the same time. But the growing group around her had launched into their own game of whodunit and scarcely noticed her after a few minutes' lively discussion. Nonetheless, Diana was enjoying herself and wished she had come backstage sooner this season, to show her lodgers that she took an interest. She was a little abashed to realize she'd never thought of that and had come for something else entirely.

"People don't kill reasonably," Paris observed. "They kill unreasonably, passionately."

Startled, Diana brought her attention back to the conversation. Who were they talking about? Then she realized that the conversation had evolved into a discussion of stage murder.

"*Witness for the Prosecution*?" Bernardo guessed.

Paris shook his head. "Not Agatha Christie."

"Not a mystery? Granville-Barker?"

"Something really obscure," Nora suggested. "Richard Vole—*The Two Mrs. Carrolls*."

"What's so obscure about that?" someone objected.

Give up?" said Paris gleefully. Obviously this was a game they often played. Diana got up to leave just as Paris announced, "*The Chalk Garden*!" to a general chorus of groans.

"Excuse me," Diana said, climbing over outstretched legs. The others, engrossed in abusing Paris for stumping them, scarcely noticed. She looked around for Nigel, but he had disappeared, and Alex had not reappeared.

Diana made for a door beyond the rehearsal stage on the far side of the room, sure that was the way they'd come in, but when she emerged into a prop room, she realized she'd picked the wrong door. She was about to retrace her steps when the sound of raised voices from the stage caught her ear.

"What, precisely, are you implying?"

It was Nigel, employing his best ruling-class accent.

"Come off it, Henson, what's it to you?"

Diana glanced around a black curtain and saw the actor who played Tybalt taking a careless yet alert stance in the pale glare of the one light that had been left on over the stage. He was an actor she did not know, except from his performances; he was talented but, she had heard, unpredictable. He looked fairly ordinary now, as he shrugged and grinned at Nigel, but she well knew that in this milieu, appearances could be deceiving.

Nigel was looking distinctly out of sorts. His normally calm demeanor had stiffened into tension, and he was scowling at the other man. This seemed only to amuse Tybalt, who made no move to back away.

"You fancy her, don't you?" he taunted. "And she probably doesn't give you a second glance."

Nigel took a step forward.

"Well, why should she?" Tybalt remarked chummily. "She's probably got her eye on bigger game."

At the same instant that Diana realized what they were talking about, Nigel took a quick step sideways and picked up a stage sword from a prop table. He advanced toward Tybalt.

"Take that back," he said in a low voice.

"What are you going to do?" Tybalt said. "Run me through?"

He didn't sound in the least intimidated, but Diana had seen those swords up close. They were made of titanium and weren't so dull that they couldn't do plenty of damage in angry hands. Yet she dared not intervene for fear of causing an accident just by startling the two men.

Tybalt snapped out of his causal stance and snatched up another sword, assuming a fencer's stance opposite Nigel.

"*En garde!*"

Nigel, angry and therefore careless, lunged at Tybalt, who sprang out of the way of his clumsy approach. He laughed, only making Nigel more furious—but less reckless. Nigel turned slowly, assessed the situation, and was about to make a second lunge when Alex quietly stepped up behind him and took his left arm in a firm grasp while disarming him with the other hand.

For an instant, Tybalt looked as if he would take unsportsmanlike advantage of his opponent's helplessness, but then Diana saw Mark Edwards watching from behind Alex. Tybalt's eyes refocused and he saw Mark too. He shrugged, laid his sword carefully back on the prop table, and silently disappeared into the recesses of the upstage darkness.

"That was stupid," Alex remarked offhandedly, as he let Nigel go and put the sword back in its place.

Nigel yanked his arm out of reach, started to say something, then seemed to think better of it and glanced toward Mark, who had said nothing up to now.

"Sorry," Nigel said. Mark only nodded, and Nigel, dismissed, slunk away.

"What do you suppose that was all about?" Mark asked.

Alex shrugged. "I think we'd better just assume they were rehearsing."

"That's all right for you to say. But now I'll have to referee as well as direct when it comes time for their Act Two duel."

"I expect they'll have gotten it out of their systems by then," Alex said.

"Let's hope so. Well, see you later, Alex. Ellen's rounding up the straying herd as we speak, and I've got notes for them."

Alex waved him off, but stood still for a moment, contemplating the prop table. Then he looked around.

"Diana?"

Unerringly, he found where she was hiding, in the shadows behind the light board. Quickly, she wiped her eyes before she rose to confront him. She hadn't been aware that she had crouched down near the floor, trying to make herself invisible.

"How did you know I was there?"

"I recognized your *Shalimar*. I hoped it wasn't Nigel wearing it."

"Don't—"

He put his arms around her, a comforting, unromantic embrace, and let her cry on his shoulder. After a minute, she pushed herself away.

"I'm sorry. It's just—you were right about Nigel. I had no idea he felt that way...."

"Don't give it too much weight," he said, almost as if he were dismissing the whole affair as insignificant, yet she knew he was concerned more about her feelings than Nigel's. "You know actors—they exaggerate everything. They over-react. They over-feel. Tomorrow Mercutio and Tybalt will be the best of friends again."

"Again?"

He laughed. "Well, maybe not. They never liked each other all that much. But their quarrel will stay on the stage now, where it belongs."

She smiled weakly up at him. "I suppose you'll see to that?"

"Not me. That's Mark's job. Let him do it."

He held her there a moment later, and when she was still again and breathing normally, he said, "What about my lunch then? I'm famished."

Chapter 18

"This way," Diana said, turning right as they left the theater, away from the center of the village. "That is, if you don't mind a bit of a walk. It's too late for lunch and too early for dinner at most of the local eating places, but The Striped Bass will probably feed us."

She had decided, on an impulse she hadn't anticipated, to let him in on one of her secrets—a tiny little inn within walking distance of the theater but not much frequented by its patrons because it didn't advertise in the program and was located down a secluded lane. The food at The Striped Bass was simple but exquisitely prepared, and the service was attentive but unhurried—a tendency which, if any theater patrons chanced to find the little inn despite its precautions, would have left them shifting anxiously in their seats as curtain time loomed. But it was ideal for quiet conversation with an interesting companion. Today Diana was in a mood for both companionship and talk, particularly with Alex.

"I'll follow you anywhere," he said, agreeably. "That is, if you won't be embarrassed to see me wolfing down my food as a result of a long wait for my supper and deprivation that I'm no longer used to."

"Augmented by the receding adrenalin rush of performance?" she guessed.

He grinned, but didn't deny it, and they said little more for the twenty-minute walk to their destination. When they entered the inn, Alex looked around interestedly, then twirled an imaginary cigar and asked in a Groucho Marx voice, "Do you come here often?"

She smiled. "I did at one time." The Striped Bass had been Daniel's favorite watering hole, but she thought she wouldn't mention that. "It's been a while."

The maître'd, obviously recognizing Alex but making no special effort to flatter him, addressed Diana instead.

"Good to see you again, Mrs. Quick. Your usual table?"

"Yes, thank you, Michel. How have you been?"

This prompted a cheerful recital about the waiter's work, family, and the state of his world generally, which somehow came to an end that didn't call for a response just as he seated them at a window table overlooking a brook and a mill wheel. It would have been too quaint had the scene been deliberately prettified and had evening not already been descending, obscuring the details until the view recalled a Rufus Porter mural.

Michel handed them menus, recited the day's specials, and took himself off. Still Alex said nothing, so Diana asked finally, "Have you been here before? If you have, lie. I'd hoped I could show you something about Middleford you didn't know."

He smiled. "No, I haven't been here, and no, I'm not lying, but I am wondering how I've missed this."

"It's a favorite with people who run B&B's and other eateries in town—sort of a busman's holiday resort where we are treated in the manner to which we aspire to treat our own guests. And the food is wonderful."

And so it proved. The bread, which came promptly, was baked on the premises and still hot from the oven. Diana's salad was enhanced by a unique house dressing; Alex's soup smelled divine. Her salmon was poached to perfection, and Alex attacked his filet mignon with enthusiasm. Their conversation, while they concentrated on their food, was limited but neither felt obliged to fill the silence. Just the act of enjoying good food together was intimate enough to be soothing but not stimulating.

Over an after-dinner espresso for Diana and a port for Alex, he said, "I've cleared Mark from suspicion in our crime, by the way. You can cross him off your suspect list."

Reluctantly, she returned to the subject of alibis. "Where was he Wednesday afternoon?"

"At one, he met with the set designer for *Duchess of Malfi* and then there was a meeting of the board of directors of the festival, at his home, until half past seven. I haven't actually confirmed this with any of the other board members, but I will if you'd like."

She shook her head. "I don't think we need bother." At this moment, she was supremely unconcerned with alibis and murderous doings.

She said nothing for a moment, expecting him to take up the matter of the other suspects, but instead he said, "You know, talking to Mark, I got the impression that he's considering leaving the festival—if they'll let him go."

She had not heard this particular rumor before, but she wasn't surprised. "He's been here for ten years. One can hardly blame him for looking for a new challenge. But who would take his place?"

"That's the big question."

He paused, and a moment later she realized what he was thinking. Her heart, unaccountably, leapt, and she felt her cheeks get warm. "You? But—you'd have to move here pretty much permanently."

He laughed. "Thank you for not being astonished that I'd be cheeky enough to think I could do the job."

"Don't be absurd. Of course you could do it. Are you considering it?"

"I might. I haven't been offered it formally. The season is young. I have time to think about it. I tell you this in confidence, of course."

"I understand." She finished her coffee and then confessed, "Speaking of the festival ... We have met before, you know. Twice in fact, although I can't imagine you'd remember the first time."

He raised an eyebrow. "I don't believe I could have forgotten either occasion. Are you sure?"

She laughed. "I think I remember better than you. I was very young, scarcely a teenager, the first time, and you were here only as a visitor. The second time was your first season and you were, I expect, trying hard to impress."

"If you refer to the festival's first season, I was indeed very green and very eager. How did we meet? Where?"

My husband—that is, my husband-to-be, as we didn't marry until twelve years later—introduced us the first time. You'd remember him—Daniel Quick. He founded the festival, and that first season I was working in the box office."

"Of course." He looked thoughtfully at her, as if trying to mentally sort his questions before asking them, but then did not ask anything after all.

"I'd known you were his widow," he said. "I suppose I just didn't connect...."

"He was twenty years my senior," she said. Somehow, perhaps because the prospect of his staying on in Middleford had come up in the way it had, she felt she had to tell him everything about herself, yet she didn't want to just recite facts. She wished he'd tell her how much he did know. Surely he had as much curiosity about her this time around as she had about him when they first met. Or did he? Was she deceiving herself?

"He was my mentor," he said, unexpectedly. "Your husband, I mean. Not that he knew he was, but he was so confident and so sure of his goals, at least as far as the festival was concerned. Yet he never stepped on anyone's toes, never threw his weight around. I couldn't have a better role model if I did decide to take on the artistic directorship."

He thought for a moment, as if searching for ideas he hadn't expressed before. "It took me some time to realize that Daniel wasn't universally liked, because while he was unfailingly polite, he never took idiocy or incompetence kindly and did not hesitate to get rid of it when it appeared. I remembered that when I began directing myself, and then my acting got better too, so long as I remembered not to put up with anything second-rate, particularly in myself."

He brought his eyes back from the now darkened view out the window and smiled at her in a way that did nothing for her accelerated heartbeat. "Obviously, he didn't settle for second-best in his private life, either."

She didn't know what to say. She ought to have been flattered, but something was wrong. She'd loved Daniel, so why should she feel mildly disappointed at Alex finding in her the same qualities Daniel had?

He seemed to sense the change in her mood and said lightly, "Are you ready to go?"

Michel had discreetly brought the bill, and Alex had discreetly paid it some time ago, but they'd been left alone until they were ready to leave—another virtue of the service at The Striped Bass, in Diana's opinion. She rose wordlessly and let him lead her to the door.

Outside, it had gotten noticeably cooler. There had been a light rain, and she shivered in the damp.

"Shall I go back and have Michel call a taxi for us?" he said.

She shook her head. "No, by the time Middleford's meager taxi service gets into action, we'll be soaked through. Let's walk back. That will warm me up, and after all that food, I need the exercise."

He lent a supporting arm as they stepped into the road, but otherwise kept a slight physical distance, as if he understood her new emotional distance. But how could he, if she didn't know the reason for it herself? Contrarily, she missed his protective closeness, but it seemed to be up to her to reestablish that connection.

She searched for a topic of conversation. She hadn't told him yet about the autopsy report, but somehow she did not want to renew that subject. Nor did she want to probe any personal corners, to ask him what had gone wrong with his marriage, for one thing, despite her curiosity about it since she'd read his biography.

"I was impressed by your performance this afternoon," she said finally, finding a more or less neutral subject.

"What performance? Oh, you mean as the Prince. Not much to it."

"It's nothing to do with its being a small part. You dominated that stage when you walked out on it. That's amazing."

"I'd have been more amazing if they'd let me ride a horse on. Don't think I didn't suggest it."

She understood from his making a joke of it that this was not something he cared to talk about. Perhaps it was something he felt outsiders, non-actors, could not appreciate. He might have been right.

They walked in silence for a while. The elms along the street south of The Inn on the Green, appropriately named Elm Street, dripped a bit from the earlier rain, and a light mist was rising. It was very quiet, a quality about Middleford that Diana appreciated. Even in the height of the tourist season, there were quiet streets and private places to get away from the midsummer crowds. If she wished to.

They approached the inn from the gatehouse side. Diana found the huge iron key that opened the old gate and let them in, replacing the key in the crook in the stone wall where it had come from.

"How long has that been there?" he asked.

She knew what he meant. "Probably more than a century. As long as I can remember, anyway."

The floodlights were still shining on the back lawn, which was just as well because it was muddier than ever around the septic works. Diana immediately saw what else was different and headed toward a white tarp covering some object near the septic diggings.

"Looks like your friend Romeo is still hard at work," Alex noted, coming up behind her and eying the canvas-covered mound.

"He said he'd be finished next week, but I haven't seen a lot of progress lately. This is new, though," she added. "He must have left something behind."

"Tools, very likely," Alex said, and obligingly lifted the tarp to look.

Diana screamed and leapt backwards. He caught her just as she slipped on the mud, then held her with her head turned into his shoulder as he took in for himself what she had seen.

"A skeleton! Well, I've heard of skeletons in one's closet—but in one's plumbing?"

His light tone soothed her somewhat, but she still did not look around. "Who is it?"

"Alas, poor Yorick, I haven't a clue," he said. "If it's any comfort, I doubt it's anyone you know. There's not a shred of—I mean, it looks quite old. No more than bleached bones."

She breathed a sigh of relief and turned to look for herself. But he headed her in the direction of the kitchen door, gently shielding her from the sight.

"There must have been an old gravesite I didn't know about on the inn grounds," she said, when he'd sat her down at the kitchen table and proceeded to make tea. "Goodness knows, anyone might have been buried there for any number of reasons over the centuries...." Her heart had stopped beating double-time, and the familiar surroundings relaxed her.

She sat down and took a deep breath. He set the tea things on the table in front of her, then handed her a note in Margo's handwriting. "This was stuck to the fridge with a magnet."

Diana unfolded the note and read aloud: "Diana— Just a warning. Vitelli's men unearthed—literally—an old skeleton when they were digging this afternoon. It's covered up. I've notified the police."

"Now she tells me," Diana complained.

"Apparently there are no missing-persons reports on file locally, or your Chief Brewster would have carted the thing to the medical examiner's office by now."

"Perhaps he was here—Dr. Sunderland, I mean. They may be very old bones indeed, in which case he'd notify the anthropology department at the nearest college. They're compiling a record of local history as revealed by artifacts that are dug up during building projects and that sort of thing. Very likely they wouldn't want it moved until they could see it where it was found. I suppose they have tests to identify old graves and such, although I didn't know we had any on the grounds. Maybe even old bones tell them something they're interested in knowing."

She was talking just to make noise in the silent night, realized it, and stopped. She half expected him to offer comfort, but he had put that distance, literally as well as figuratively this time, between them again. Nonetheless, he asked, from across the room, "Will you be all right alone tonight?"

She stood up and moved next to him. "Hold me, please, Alex."

He rose and obliged, but obviously with reluctance.

"What's wrong?" she said.

"I'm sorry, Diana. I just realized tonight that you're looking for something I'm not sure I want to give."

"I don't understand." His arms felt so good around her, even the slight pressure of his cheek against hers warming her through and through, that she wanted to get as close as she could. Already she could feel the warmth spreading inside her and her imagination raced ahead, looking for heat, and passion. She hadn't felt that in a long time.

But then he lifted her chin, and she opened her eyes to find him searching her face. She didn't know what he expected to find. "I want to be more than a refuge for you, Diana. I want to give you more than comfort. I don't want you to think of me as just a successor to Daniel."

She did want more, she knew now, but stupidly she pushed him away and stepped back. "You don't know anything about my relationship to Daniel!"

"I don't know much, no. I do know what's stayed with you. You may still need that, and I will give it gladly—but not if that's all you'll take from me."

He was right, she understood now, with a sinking heart. Like Daniel, Alex represented security, comfort—a refuge, as he'd called it. But while it was enough for Daniel—she had thought—it obviously was not for Alex.

But she wanted more, too. Didn't she? Suddenly she realized why she had pulled away from him in the restaurant, when he'd seemed to be seeing the same things in her that Daniel had. Again her imagination had gotten ahead of her willingness to go a step further, to exchange her need to be protected, to follow his lead in all things in return for a fuller love, with real passion and partnership. Of course simple comforts weren't enough for him; he'd been looking for something else. Apparently he hadn't found it, and that thought hurt.

"Go, then! I don't need that from you. I—I'll get it from Nigel."

"Don't," he said softly.

He was right. That would be cruel.

In the end, she didn't look for Nigel. She went to bed alone and slept from emotional exhaustion more than fatigue.

Chapter 19

The next morning, Diana was surprised to find herself having a rational discussion with Beth Hudson about the possible origin of the skeleton that even now was the focus of attention of half-a-dozen anthropology students ringed around the hole in the lawn.

"I don't suppose you got a good look at it?" Beth asked, sipping coffee in a chair facing Diana's on the verandah. The day had dawned sunny and almost summerlike, to the delight of the professor from the state university whom Kent Brewster had called in to assess the skeleton before it was moved from where it had been found. At the moment, Dr. Leakey—as Beth insisted on calling him, although he didn't look like any Leakey Diana had ever met—was lecturing to his students in what Beth no doubt considered an annoyingly inaudible whisper. Beth, like Diana, had been asked to stay back out of the way, and her press credentials afforded her no more access than did Diana's technical ownership of the grave and its contents by virtue of their being found in her backyard.

"It was dark," she said in response to Beth's question, "but ... "

Beth raised an inquiring eyebrow.

"But I snuck out this morning before all of them"— she pointed her chin at the group around the site—"got here." She grinned triumphantly.

Beth made applause motions, but instead of asking for details, said, "Does this come under the heading of getting back on the horse after you've been thrown?"

"Something like that. I thought that if I'm going to go on stumbling over dead bodies, I'd better get used to it. Although ... "

Beth waited for it this time.

"A skeleton isn't someone you'd know," was the best way Diana could describe her lack of emotional connection to the skeleton.

"What did it look like, then?"

"White. Rather small. There was nothing left to indicate who it belonged to, at least not that I could see."

"I guess that's what that gang are here to decide," Beth said, looking like a younger sister resentful at being kept out of her brothers' tree house.

Diana stirred her coffee absently and contemplated why she hadn't reacted the same way last night as she had when she'd stumbled over Bradford Gray's body in the old burying ground. This wasn't someone she knew, of course—at least, she hoped not. But her imagination wasn't working overtime to come up with a story about how the skeleton came to be buried in her yard. Of course, last night, her imagination had been otherwise engaged, but even in the light of day, she didn't particularly care about the find in her yard, beyond a mild curiosity and a milder annoyance that the septic wouldn't be finished on time—again.

"Dr. Leakey"—a short, middle-aged man with crew-cut white hair who wore an unbuttoned lab coat—detached himself from his coterie and headed for the verandah, a grin on his face.

"Well," Beth said, sotto voce, "what do you suppose he's found?"

"Civil War!" trumpeted the professor, ascending the two steps to the verandah. He might as well have shouted, "Eureka!" Beth was trying not to giggle, and Diana reminded herself that she was the hostess here and reached for the coffeepot with a politely enquiring smile at the professor, who blithely ignored it.

Beth asked, "Do you mean the skeleton dates to the Civil War?"

"Precisely," said the professor.

"Can you tell that from just the skeleton?"

"Not even," he said, finally noticing the cup of coffee that was being held out to him and accepting it. "Button."

Both women stared at him. He pulled something out of his lab-coat pocket and showed it to them. It was a button, all right—dented metal, unusable for its original purpose now, but certainly a button.

"Civil War era," he said, after gulping down half a cup of coffee at once. He eyed the pound cake that had been invitingly sliced on a plate but not yet breached. Diana put a slice on a napkin and handed it to him.

"Thank you." He consumed the cake unhurriedly while his audience waited in anticipation of further details. "In fact," he said at last, "this button is a type that was used almost exclusively on Civil War uniforms—Army of the Potomac, I shouldn't be surprised to learn. With any luck, we'll be able to pinpoint the regiment. Even better if we find his boots or, with luck, a belt buckle."

Apparently having exhausted himself with such a long speech, the professor finished his coffee and hustled back to his dig.

Beth looked at Diana. "There's a meeting of the Historical Society tonight," she said. "Want to come?"

"Wouldn't miss it for the world."

Chapter 20

It had been years since Diana last attended a meeting of the Middleford Historical Society, even though she was a member. All "original" residents of Middleford—which was to say, anyone whose ancestors had settled there before 1750—were automatically made "founding" members, which Diana had at first considered a compliment, but later came to view as stifling, and she had stopped attending meetings. The Society, she realized, cared less about history than about heritage—theirs. Annoying anomalies, such as local families who kept slaves or prominent persons who were descended from an illegitimate line, were rarely acknowledged and never discussed.

In this light, Diana admitted to an unworthy curiosity to see what the Society would make of the newly discovered skeleton in her closet—or at least her lawn.

The bones had been carefully, almost lovingly, treated by the professor and his students, packed up, and carted away for further study, leaving her back lawn much as it had looked the day before—which was to say, messy. Diana had immediately called Vitelli's Plumbing to warn Romeo about the disruption and ask him to come over immediately to try to get the work back on schedule.

"Diana, dear!" Larraine Brewster greeted her when she entered the hall behind the library where the Society met regularly every third Tuesday of the month.

"Kent told me the exciting news—is it really a Civil War relic?"

"The skeleton?"

"The button, of course," said Larraine, as if anyone could think of anything else. Coming into the room behind Diana, Beth snickered, then covered her rudeness with a cough. Diana kicked her ankle.

"Of course," Diana agreed.

"Did you see it, Diana? Was it authentic?"

"Well, I must assume the professor is correct that it is indeed an authentic relic. I'm afraid it looked like no more than a dented piece of metal to me, but of course I'm not the expert that you are."

"Metal!" Larraine exclaimed, apparently deaf to flattery. "How exciting. Do sit down, and as soon as everyone is here, you can tell us all about it."

Diana remembered her original reservations about the Society and was struck with second thoughts about having come. She appealed to Beth.

"Do something," she whispered. "Interview somebody. Research your article."

"Chicken," Beth whispered back.

However, when push came to shove, Beth did take over, telling the story of how the skeleton had been unearthed—with some discreet omissions—and what the professor had said about it, with a few embellishments. As she had doubtless calculated, the Society members swallowed these whole.

Careful mental editing of the spirited discussion that followed yielded Diana the information that seventy-five men from Middleford had served in the Civil War over its four years—which she knew—of whom twenty had died in action. Not a bad ratio, all things considered. Ten of those heroes, she learned, rested in the old burying ground, the rest having been interred where they fell. Forty of the veterans came home and died natural deaths in the fullness of life, in their own beds.

She did some quick mental arithmetic and wondered what had happened to the other fifteen men. Did they not come home? Were they buried unidentified in a mass grave? Were the records simply lost?

Then it occurred to her. Perhaps they had deserted. It would be like the Society to strike the names of any such traitors from its rolls and deny them even the very earth they had been born from. Who could they have been? Could one of them have been her unwelcome skeletal visitor?

While Beth answered questions, and asked even more, Diana looked around to see who was there who might be able to enlighten her, candidly, about Middleford's Civil War veterans. Millie Goodall was in attendance, looking enthralled by what was being said but taking no part. Frances Burnell, wife of Bill, sat off to the side and said little—*much like her husband at board meetings*, Diana thought. She wondered what she could say to Fran that would bring up her whereabouts on the day Brad Gray died. Her heart sank at the prospect; she just couldn't do it again. Beth would have to, or Jane.

Diana realized that her never-abundant courage was flagging again, so she continued her survey. Cynthia Howell, surprisingly, was taking notes. It was rare that anyone under thirty attended Historical Society meetings; Diana decided to ask Cynthia how long she had been coming. Perhaps that would lead to something.

Just behind Cynthia sat a woman Diana had never seen before. In her mid-forties perhaps, she was certainly attractive, her red hair neatly coiffed but her makeup perhaps a little excessive for the occasion.

"Who's that?" she whispered to Beth over cookies and tea after the question-and-answer period was over. Beth looked, under cover of helping herself to another homemade butterscotch cookie—recipe from *The Society Cookbook*, available from any member for only $14.95 to benefit the Society's fund to buy books and other records to do with Middleford history.

Beth turned back to Diana, grinning.

"That's Ben's latest girlfriend, Ginger Barnes. Wonder how she got invited?"

"Ben *McIlvey*?"

"None other. I guess Fran Burnell brought her. She's an Original—Fran, I mean—so they couldn't very well refuse her guest."

"I didn't know Ben had a girlfriend—although she's hardly a girl."

"*Meow*. She's a divorcée. She and her husband bought a house from Ben out in that new Charcoal Ridge subdivision a couple of years ago. Well, wouldn't you know the husband ran off with some bimbo and Ginger got the house in the divorce settlement, but probably not much else. She's very careful about what she wears and how she keeps herself, but if she's bought any new clothes in the last year, it's because Ben paid for them."

Fascinated, Diana wondered if Jane knew about this, and why she hadn't mentioned it. Then she remembered that Jane had been married once, briefly, and divorced, and she was perpetually short on money. No doubt she would have sympathized with Ginger. Diana felt a little ashamed of her rampant curiosity, and it came back to her why she had little indulged in gossip before Brad Gray's death. Before Alex Gordon came into her life. It was too addicting.

"I suppose that will account for Ben's lying to me," she said, without realizing she'd said it aloud.

"Lying about what?" Beth said.

Diana took her aside and gave her a brief account of her conversation with Ben McIlvey and his unexpected—and slightly fishy—offer to buy her cabin at the lake, at the end of which they both stared at Ginger thoughtfully.

"I don't suppose you'd like to follow up on this?" Diana said.

"Sure, why not. *Are* you going to sell the cottage?"

"I don't know yet."

Just then, the president of the Society, Loretta Bonning Chase, approached them. "Diana, how nice to see you again. How long has it been since you last attended a meeting?"

"Too long," Diana conceded. "Thank you for allowing me to come." She smiled graciously at Loretta with just the amount of abasement in her manner to soothe the president's sensibilities. Beth rolled her eyes, an unwise gesture that Diana suspected Loretta had not missed.

"And ... Beth," Loretta said. "Such an interesting presentation. All speculation, of course, but fascinating to contemplate."

Beth rose to the bait, something she delighted in doing. "Speculation?"

"You don't really think the skeleton is Civil War era, do you?"

"I'm only reporting what the professor told us."

"But how can he tell? That button Larraine is so fascinated with ... that might have nothing to do with the skeleton. Perhaps if there had been other evidence or clothing...."

She paused and looked Beth up and down. Beth was in gypsy mode tonight, her dark hair tied up with a red ribbon, a long red tunic hanging over a green broomstick skirt and black boots. Diana thought she looked stunning, but Loretta shivered delicately.

"Nonetheless, a most enjoyable discussion. Thank you, Beth."

She sailed away, looking more than ever like Mrs. Shinn in *The Music Man*. She lacked only a bustle.

"Well," Diana said, "I guess that puts us in our place."

Beth laughed. "I think we know our place better than Loretta knows hers."

It was an astute observation. Beth might look and act flighty, but her sharp mind not only retained details but was able to place them in a bigger picture. Beth was talented; Diana wondered if she was truly content simply to run the local newspaper, which couldn't be much of a challenge for her.

"Let me know if you talk to Ben again," Beth said. "I guess I'll go grill Cynthia now."

She went off to do so, and Diana's eyes found Larraine Brewster again. She studied the woman she had known most of her life and began to realize that Larraine had changed ... recently? Diana had known, in the general way that everyone in town did, that Larraine had not been well, but no one knew for sure exactly what was wrong with her. She was actually prettier than she had been in her youth, but in a more delicate, almost fragile way. Her smile was as sweet as ever, but it came and went fleetingly, even as she chatted animatedly with Millie Goodall about the Society cookbook. Her blue eyes were less alive, and as she listened to Millie, Diana saw them waver, then go blank, then refocus on Millie, as if to do so was a physical effort.

She tried to recall how old Larraine was now. She had been in high school when Diana was still in first or second grade, before she had been sent away to boarding school, so Larraine must be nine or ten years older. She wasn't all that old, then; nor did she look her age, having kept her slim figure and being either fortunate in her natural ash-blond hair or in her choice of hairdresser. Yet, there was that vagueness, that emptiness behind the eyes....

Hesitantly, she approached Larraine and invited her to visit her at home and renew their acquaintance.

"Diana, dear, I'd love to. I'll call soon, I promise. By the way, do you have a copy of the cookbook?" She placed one in Diana's hands and opened the pages, as if helping a child to read. "There are some wonderful recipes for tea cakes and sandwiches, which would be just the thing for your hotel, don't you think?"

"I'm sure they would, Larraine. I'd be happy to buy a cookbook."

As Diana wrote out a check, she asked casually, "How is Kent now, Larraine? I know he was friends with Brad Gray and I'm sure quite upset about his death."

Diana looked up as she handed Larraine her check and was startled to see quite a different look in Larraine's eyes. It was speculative and perfectly lucid, as if she were wondering at Diana's motives for asking. But the look vanished as soon as it appeared, replaced by a wary one. She glanced away as she placed Diana's check carefully in a tin cash box.

"He loses himself in his work. I'm sure you know that with the start of the festival season, and all the new people in town, he's very busy. I keep telling him he needs to hire more deputies, but the town won't give him enough money for it. Not that there's much real crime, of course, just young people being rowdy. In fact, he had to go and break up a fight somewhere out by the lake, at some bar, the same day that Brad died. I think he believes that if he'd been nearer by, he might have found Brad somehow and maybe gotten him to a hospital before ... in time."

"He shouldn't blame himself," Diana said.

Larraine looked at her. "You're right. That's what I keep telling him. He can't blame himself. Accidents happen."

It seemed obvious to Diana that Larraine no longer had any more fond feelings for Bradford Gray than anyone else in Middleford—except Kent Brewster.

"Time will help," she said, although the cliché rang hollowly in her ears.

"Diana, you're interested in our Civil War history, aren't you?" Larraine asked suddenly, as if they hadn't been discussing skeletons and buttons only an hour ago. "I have something that may interest you related to our local history of that era." She lowered her voice, as if to prevent anyone else with a historical interest from hearing. "It's a diary. Quite fascinating. May I bring it to show you?"

"Of course. I'd be interested in seeing it."

"Is Monday all right?" Larraine persisted.

"Of course," Diana repeated. "About four o'clock?" She'd have to get Margo to make something out of *The Society Cookbook* for the occasion.

Larraine squeezed her hand and said in a tone of girlish confidences, "Thank you, dear."

Diana and Beth left together ten minutes later and compared notes as they walked home. They agreed to cross everyone at the meeting off their list, which was fine with Diana. At least for tonight, she was more inclined to indulge in history than mystery, and since Larraine had been so secretive about her diary, she did not mention their conversation to Beth. She asked instead what Beth knew about what she was beginning to think of as The Missing Fifteen.

"It's true, I'm sure, that some of our brave boys did desert," Beth told her. "They *were* just boys, you know, some of them volunteered into service by their families who needed their army wages more than they needed another mouth to feed. I imagine they were all scared, just being away from home for the first time."

"It sounds as if you've done some research on this."

"I have, for any good it's done me. That's not all that went on. Families on the other end of the socioeconomic scale of the times, who could afford it, paid the draft board to find substitutes to go to war in place of their precious sons. That didn't give them any more incentive to fight than fear or poverty.

"Of course," she added, "I can't put any of this in the *Citizen*. Someone in the Historical Society is bound to claim anyone I name in that kind of context as an ancestor and sue me for defamation."

"You could write a book."

Beth grinned. "I could write volumes about this town and never go further back in history than the start of the Festival."

Chapter 21

Her conversation with Larraine Brewster still preying on her mind, Diana threw her favorite denim jacket on over her T-shirt and jeans and went to talk to Jane Wagner about it the afternoon following the Historical Society meeting. After giving her a blow-by-blow account of the entire meeting over tea and fresh brownies, Diana described Larraine's odd behavior.

"The whole conversation begins to seem curiouser and curiouser the more I think about it," she said.

"You think she made it a point of giving Kent an alibi for The Night in Question?" Jane had taken to using that phrase as if it were capitalized; Diana had accused her of learning this from D.C. Dickson, a charge Jane heartily accepted. "The way Ben tried to give himself one?"

Diana had told Jane about her encounter with Ben McIlvey, although not yet about Ginger Barnes. Beth had said, when Diana had called her that morning to invite her to come to Jane's too, that she wanted to be present for this revelation, and she'd not yet arrived. Diana poured a third cup of Earl Grey. Neither had she yet revealed to Jane that D.C. Dickson preferred good black English Breakfast tea with plenty of milk.

"Perhaps I've just been thinking too much along those lines," Diana admitted. "Everyone seems to have an alibi, so why not Kent, I guess."

"*Does* everyone have an alibi? Can we check Ben's out? Remember, the autopsy put the time of death much earlier than we'd first thought." Jane restored herself with another brownie, and Diana wondered how she stayed so slim. Potting greenhouse plants must use up more calories than she thought. "Maybe we should review the list again."

Diana had come prepared and produced the computer printout she'd updated earlier that morning.

"I'm impressed," Jane said, looking it over. "Well, let's see then. What times are we looking at again?"

"From about four in the afternoon Wednesday. Last Wednesday." *Good heavens*, Diana thought, *had it really been only a week?* "Until seven o'clock."

"Right. So Seth Howell was having dinner with his daughter at the Colonial Café—have you ever had their chicken cacciatore, by the way? It's wonderful—from a little after five until it was time for Seth to leave for Town Hall for the Zoning Commission meeting. Hmmm ... long dinner. Are you sure?"

Diana had made a second trip to the café that morning for a hearty breakfast and a confidential chat with the counter help. "The waitress remembered Seth and Cynthia because of the time they spent there. They were playing a game of chess, which she thought was a strange dinner-time amusement, and they wanted to finish it."

"Obliging of them," Jane remarked, then backtracked. "Not that I'd ever have suspected either Seth or Cynthia, mind you. He's my hero."

"You mean he *was*," Diana teased. "Until D.C. Dickson came along."

"What can I say. I'm fickle. Who's next? On the list, I mean."

"The obvious suspect—Marjorie Gray. She clearly had a facial, but how do we know she was hiding it at home all that time? Or that she didn't have an accomplice who hauled away the body after she'd murdered Brad in his own rec room?" Diana had allowed her imagination free rein with Marjorie.

"That room has a wet bar, I found out," Jane said. "*And* a pool table. That room alone is bigger than my whole first floor."

"How do you know that? About the pool table, I mean."

"I went up there to pay my condolence call on Marjorie—at a time when I knew she wouldn't be home."

"Very clever. Who gave you a tour of the house?"

"The maid, Corelle. It so happens that she cleaned for me when I first opened Willow Lane Cottage. She came cheap then, but it was an awful lot of work, so as soon as this place got to the point that I could run it myself, she quit. I gave her a good reference, and we're still friends. Now I guess she likes the long down-times she gets working for Marjorie. Except when Marjorie wants something, of course—then she has to hustle.

"Anyway, we caught up on old times, and she offered to show me around, since I'd never been in the house before. You couldn't have dragged me there, even if I'd been invited, but that's neither here nor there. In the course of the conversation, Corelle let drop that Marjorie had indeed been home all of Wednesday. She remembered because she couldn't even go home to cook her husband's dinner in case she missed Marjorie's summons—and apparently she summoned a lot that day. She was just coming off her painkillers, which turned *her* into a pain."

"So we can thank Corelle for a useful bit of information." Diana made a check mark next to Marjorie's name on the list and tried not to sound disappointed.

"Don't forget to cross the Goodalls off too," Jane said, leaning over to point at the next names on Diana's list. "Even if they weren't in Bennington, I'd be willing to let them off."

"Why?"

"Motive, means, and opportunity, remember? It doesn't matter if they have the opportunity if they don't have means or motive—and either everyone on your list has that, or no one does. But as for the means, Andy may look healthy, but he's got terrible arthritis. I doubt he could swing a piece of marble or anything else hard enough to kill anyone, or even push a younger, stronger man that hard. And Millie's tiny; she wouldn't have the strength either."

"I suppose you're right," Diana said. Physical fragility would have seemed like flimsy evidence were it applied to anyone high on her suspect list, but the Goodalls were there only because no one could confirm their whereabouts Wednesday afternoon. If she'd kept the list current, Diana realized, it could be a good deal shorter by now. Did that mean they were closing in on an answer? She certainly didn't feel any more confident that she had a week ago.

But she said, "And it turns out that Mark Edwards was in a meeting all of that afternoon with the set designer for *Duchess*, and then with the theater's board of directors, which no doubt numerous witnesses would testify to."

"*Duchess,* eh? Aren't we being theatrical. Next you'll be talking about *Cats Hamburg* and *Cats Tokyo* like that lighting man—what was his name?—who stayed with me last summer before flitting off again to some other overseas production of *Cats*. If he hadn't been here for a different show, I'd think he made a career of *Cats*."

Diana smiled, remembering that the lighting designer in question had been Jane's hero last summer.

"One can, I hear. It's still playing somewhere every day. Where were we?"

"Nigel Henson," said Jane, pointing.

Diana had forgotten he was still on the list but, reminded of the motives Alex had ascribed to Nigel as a reason to add him to it, she was disinclined to get into a discussion about him. His infatuation with her no longer seemed even remotely a joke. Jane seemed to sense her reluctance and obligingly assumed he'd have been at the theater too, with Mark Edwards and company, Wednesday afternoon. Indeed, all the theater people could provide alibis for each other, if pressed, so there was no reason to keep any of them on the list. She crossed off the Burnells too, on the admittedly shaky grounds that Bill would likely have been backstage and Fran at her part-time job in the box office.

"Which still leaves Ben McIlvey," she went on.

"Leaves Ben McIlvey where?" came a voice from the Dutch door. "To heaven and to those arrows that prick and sting him?"

Diana and Jane turned to see Beth Hudson, simply dressed for a change in jeans and a festival T-shirt, leaning over the Dutch door. Jane got up to unlatch the bottom half, and Diana remarked that she was beginning to sound like the actors, but they'd never quote from *Hamlet*. Too easy. Beth ignored that.

"Sounds like I missed the beginning of the meeting," she said. "Why didn't you wait for me? I'm a busy person, you know. The news won't wait." She sounded remarkably cheery, which set Jane on her bah-humbug track.

"Sorry," she said. "If we'd known you needed an invitation to show up on time, we'd have sent one."

Beth sat down, poured tea for herself, and asked Diana, "Did you tell her about the meeting last night, about Ben?"

"Ben McIlvey was at the Historical Society meeting?" Jane said, incredulous. I don't believe it."

"He wasn't," Diana explained. "But Ginger was."

Jane looked baffled, and Diana felt absurdly delighted to know some gossip that Jane hadn't heard. Beth gestured for her to tell all.

"Ben's lady friend," she told Jane.

"No! How long has this been going on?"

They speculated happily on where this relationship might lead until Jane asked, sensibly, "But how does Ginger affect Ben's alibi?"

"I don't know," Diana admitted. "If he was with her, he might not be willing to say so publicly, which would look bad. If any of this became public, anyway."

"Maybe if we went to Ginger and told her flat out that Ben could be implicated in Brad's death, she'd fess up?"

Diana and Beth looked dubious, so Jane retracted her idea.

"So Ben is still on the possibles list," Jane said, getting up to add hot water to the teapot. "What next?"

"I think we should decide what we actually know and see if we can draw any conclusions from that," Beth suggested.

"You probably know more than we do together," Diana said. "Facts, I mean, as opposed to speculation, which seems to be all I, for one, have been able to produce."

"Tell us more about the autopsy first," Jane said to Beth, as she topped off her and Diana's mugs. "You've seen the actual document?"

"Yes. It's in the record room at Town Hall and open to anyone, but I wasn't allowed to photocopy it, goodness knows why. Doris Mallory said she didn't know either, but until she was told differently, those were the rules."

"Odd," said Diana.

"But what did it say?" Jane persisted. "You took notes, didn't you?"

"Extensively. Brad was killed by a blow to the skull, resulting in—let me see if I remember this—a basilar skull fracture. I asked a doctor about this, and apparently Brad was hit on the one particularly vulnerable place on the human skull. You could fall and injure yourself there by accident, though, so it's no proof of murder, certainly not of any anatomical knowledge."

Jane sighed and raised baffled eyebrows at Diana, who said, "All right. Fact One. Brad died from a blow to the head, not a fall—wait a minute. Don't autopsies specify a 'means' *and* a 'cause' of death, or at least an immediate cause and underlying causes? For example, a stroke may kill you, but coronary artery disease precipitated the stroke."

"Yes," Beth confirmed. "But the report said 'probable' accident, which gets us no further. That's been the general assumption all along."

"What else do we know for sure?" Jane prompted.

"We know that a skeleton was found in Diana's back yard," Beth offered with a grin. Jane dismissed this as a consideration.

"Let's concentrate on Brad's movements," she suggested. "If we can figure out where he was every moment that Wednesday afternoon, maybe we can pinpoint when and where he was killed."

"Died," Diana said, persisting in keeping the facts to the fore. "As far as we still know, and the autopsy says, he wasn't murdered."

"Killjoy," muttered Jane.

"All right," Diana said. "I'll set up a computer file to track his movements and fill in what we know so far; then we'll have to do some more investigating. But what about his car?" she added. "Do we know where that disappeared to? We still don't know why he walked through the burying ground that night."

"Yes!" Jane exclaimed. "I forgot—the car was parked on Long Ridge Avenue all afternoon."

"Says who?" Beth asked. Jane reiterated her conversation with Corelle.

"Brad lived on Long Ridge," Diana said. "But why park it in the street? He has a garage, and a driveway, which is where I'd park if I were going to be using the car again the same day."

That produced a thoughtful silence. "It does seem odd, doesn't it?" Beth said. "How did he get to the burying ground? Or how did his body get there?"

"Jane, are you sure Corelle said the car was on the street all day?"

"Well, it was there the three or four times she looked out the window. She couldn't remember when she did that, exactly."

Another silence. "Well, that's not very conclusive," Beth said. "Jane, do you think Corelle would talk to me? I guess I can find some excuse to interview her. And she'd know when Brad was home during the day, which would be a start."

"Just make sure Marjorie's not home when you do," Jane said.

Beth nodded. "I've already been to the real estate office, but as you know, Brad didn't spend a lot of time at a desk."

This reminded Diana of her visit, and she told them about Ben's takeover of Brad's office, which amused them for several minutes.

Then Jane said, "I just had another thought about motive. Maybe whoever did it didn't intend to. Maybe someone just got mad. Goodness knows, that was more than likely any day Brad went anywhere. Who has a temper?"

"Who'd move the body and fake an accident scene, if the death was a real accident to begin with? Why not just report it?" Beth asked. No one had an answer to this.

"Let's go on," Diana suggested. "Who saw Brad last? Do we know?"

"He was in his office from one to three, according to his secretary," Beth said.

"That wasn't in the police report," Diana said, making a note. She'd begun a new list on the back of the print-out she'd brought with her, headed *Brad's movements*.

"No, why would it be? I got it from the horse's mouth. Helen said that Brad had an appointment with a builder at four, out on a site in the new Hickory Ridge development, and she assumed he was heading out there when he left the office."

"Well, that accounts for a good chunk of his day," Jane said, "but it doesn't take an hour to get from his office to Hickory Ridge. Did he go somewhere else first? Was he driving his Beamer at the time?"

"Did he actually get there?" Diana asked. There were still more questions than answers, she reflected, discouraged.

"I don't know," Beth admitted. "I guess that could be important...."

Beth's cell phone rang just as she promised to talk to Helen again. She cut herself off abruptly, saying into the phone, "Are you sure? Anyone we know? Okay, I'll get over to headquarters and find out. Hold the presses."

"I've always wanted to say that," she said to Jane and Diana's expectant looks as she closed her phone, but her smile was far from the cheerful grin she'd worn when she arrived.

"There's been another ... body," she said finally.

"Oh, my God!" Jane said. "Who? Anyone we know?"

"Not identified yet, Charlie claims. It was found out by Mirror Lake, by hikers. It had apparently been there for a while."

Beth sighed, got up from her chair and, snagging an extra brownie for the road, said, "I'll keep you posted. Don't tell anyone anything yet, until we find out something official."

When Beth left, she seemed to take the energy out of the room. Even Jane sat staring out the window, scarcely noticing that their tea had grown cold. Diana roused herself and scraped back her chair.

"I'd better go, Jane. See you soon?"

Jane smiled. "How about tomorrow? I guess we'd better finish this discussion, since we don't seem to have come to any conclusions today. Not to mention that this news may shed a whole new light on things."

"All right. But come to my house. The opening of *Romeo and Juliet* is fast approaching, and the house will be chaos, but we can use the gatehouse."

No sooner were the words out of her mouth than Diana mentally kicked herself. Did Jane know that Alex had moved out the day after the skeleton turned up? Could she convince her that it would have happened any day anyway, since his rental house had been hurriedly made ready for him, the occupants happy to set sail early for the sake of an extra week's rent?

But if Jane guessed what she was thinking, or had any inkling about what had happened between Diana and Alex, she didn't show it.

"Sounds good. Will you give us lunch? If we get there at noon, we'll be out of your way in time for you to get gussied up for the big night."

Jane got up to see her out. Diana paused at the door.

"Jane ... have you talked to Larraine Brewster lately?"

"Not for a couple of weeks, why?"

"Go see her if you can. I don't think she's well, but I didn't want to ask when I saw her at the Historical Society meeting. It's not something I can put finger on. She looks perfectly well, but she's ... well, never mind what I think. See for yourself, if you can."

"I'll make a point of it."

"Bye, Jane. Thanks for the tea."

Chapter 22

It didn't take long for the news to be all over town, even before the next edition of the *Weekly Citizen* was delivered. Police headquarters was besieged, and Charlie Pettibone didn't know which phone line to answer first, or which citizen to let in to ask questions he didn't have the authority to answer, even if he knew the answer.

He was mightily relieved, Diana heard later, when Chief Brewster got there and announced to everyone that he would hold a meeting at the Town Hall that evening to tell them what he knew and answer all their questions then. For now, the investigation was ongoing, and he couldn't speculate until they had more information. When no one in the crowd of citizens seemed inclined to move, he closed the door in their faces.

Diana heard this from Jane, who was one of the first in line at police headquarters, and called Diana to be sure she would attend the "press conference," as she called it. Diana wasn't at all sure she wanted to hear about another murder, if that was what it was, but when Jane assured her that it must have been strangers involved this time, based on the simple fact that no one they knew had been missing for "a while," as Beth had described the time of death. That was the only exclusive information they had, so Diana agreed to go with her, if Jane met her at the inn, from where it was an easy walk to Town Hall.

The meeting room wasn't as packed as Diana had expected, given the sensational news. Maybe everyone else had checked for missing friends as well and found none, so lost interest. Somewhat relieved by this, Diana found her curiosity growing again. She hoped she wasn't getting addicted to murder cases … *if* this was another one, she kept telling herself, which they didn't know yet.

Kent came into the room promptly on the hour he'd promised and stood at the table usually occupied by some town board or another. Two selectmen followed him in, sat down, and looked attentive but uninvolved. Charlie Pettibone looked out the door for any stragglers, then closed it and stood at attention with his back to the door.

"We've identified the body," Kent said, getting right to the point. "It's Jackson Miller."

There was a light murmur from the audience, but no outcries of any kind. Kent looked, Diana thought, both regretful and relieved.

"I see that most of you didn't know Mr. Miller by name," he said, "but you'll have seen him around town. He was homeless, but harmless. He usually slept in a tent in the woods by the lake, but he walked around town during the day, taking whatever handouts people wanted to give him."

This elicited collective nods of recognition. Jackson Miller had clearly been down on his luck, although no one knew why or how he had made his way to Middleford, nor did most of them ever learn his name. His ragged clothing was always neat and his beard trimmed, however inexpertly. He never approached anyone for money, but he had a habit of checking the *New York Times* sales boxes on the Green for change left in the slots, and people had taken to surreptitiously leaving some when they saw him coming. Diana had left sandwiches in her mailbox for him when she or Margo spotted him from one of her upper windows. By night he was always gone, leaving not so much as a paper napkin behind. There must have been a sad story behind his presence in Middleford, and now Diana wished she'd known it. She'd ask Beth what she knew. Surely there was a story in that lonely life.

"We're trying to locate his family," Kent went on, "but so far it doesn't look like he had any. He'll be buried in Potter's Field if we don't catch a break that way."

"How did he die, Chief?" Beth asked, getting to what everyone wanted to know.

Kent hesitated. "He was beaten to death."

A gasp came from the listeners, then a hubbub of low-pitched conversation that Kent let go on for a few minutes, until a voice from the back of the room that Diana didn't recognize said, "Why would anyone kill a harmless old man, Chief? Do we have a serial killer on our hands?"

Louder comments broke out all around. Kent raised his hand until the noise died down and looked toward the anonymous voice with an angry scowl—or as close to angry as Kent ever got.

"No," he said unhesitatingly. "A fifty-dollar bill, with traces of heroin on it, was found in one of Mr. Miller's pockets, so we're investigating whether drugs were somehow involved and he died because of some argument about them, or he stumbled on a deal going down. It's been known to happen in those woods at all times of the year."

Diana thought the stumbling on a drug deal scenario more likely. She could not imagine Jackson having anything to do with dealing drugs, however hard up he was. Like most supposedly perfect towns, Middleford had its secret drug subculture, but it had never come out in the open and no one had ever been caught selling drugs, probably because the high school was small and few secrets survived among teenagers who had known each other since they were toddlers. She hoped that wouldn't ever change. More of the adults, at least those who could afford it, probably used drugs, but Diana didn't know anyone who did, nor did she care to.

Kent took a deep breath and added, "If you're trying to make a connection with the recent untimely death of one of our leading citizens—don't. There is no connection. There have been no other deaths in the state similar to Mr. Miller's. It was clearly a crime of opportunity, unpremeditated, and I'll thank you, whoever asked that question, to not spread such speculation around."

Kent answered a few more questions, but the meeting broke up quickly, since the victim this time was a relative stranger, and life in Middleford could go on its placid way. Diana realized that everyone but herself, Jane, Beth, and Alex must have accepted the official story about Brad Gray's death and had no inkling that it might have been something else. Clearly, she and her fellow investigators were isolating themselves rather than looking for the "truth" for the good of the town.

Outside Town Hall, she waited for Jane and Beth to catch up to share this realization with them. They approached her together, Beth no longer showing any signs of eagerness to rush off and "stop the presses."

"So a body is no longer front-page news?" Diana asked, trying not to sound accusatory.

Beth smiled, guessing what she was thinking. "The story's already ninety-percent written. Kent gave me all the information he had this morning after I promised not to say anything to anybody until after his announcement. Which meant I had to write the whole story myself, at home, and not get my typesetter involved until the last minute. Of course, I now have to add the quotes from tonight's meeting."

"Do you know anything about Jackson Miller?" Jane asked, taking the words out of Diana's mouth.

"Not much," Beth admitted. "But I'm giving him a nice obit. People looked kindly on him in general, I think."

"What was all that about a serial killer?" Diana asked.

Jane looked abashed and confessed, "I bribed my handyman to come here and ask that. I wanted to see if it would make Kent admit to anything fishy about Brad's death. That's still the million-dollar question, isn't it? And now, the additional question of whether there's any connection between the two deaths."

Beth and Diana looked at her in astonishment.

"I don't know whether to be appalled or admire your cleverness," Diana said.

"It didn't work, though, did it?" Beth said. "He didn't say anything remotely revealing."

Jane sighed. "No, and I need to do some more thinking about all this. Shall we meet again tomorrow? Beth?"

"Not until I put the paper to bed."

"Diana?"

"I'll call you," Diana waffled. "I'm too tired to think about it right now."

With that, Beth said good night and strode purposefully off. Jane was in no hurry and wandered off murmuring, 'When shall we three meet again, in thunder, lightning, or in rain…?'"

Chapter 23

Diana spent the next morning working furiously at whatever manual labor she could find to do at the inn, not picking up her phone to call Jane or, especially, Alex, and not listening for a knock on the door. If there were calls or knocks, she didn't hear them.

After lunch, however, she abruptly left Margo supervising the hanging of wallpaper in two potential guest rooms and headed for the library. She'd lose herself in research, she decided, to take her mind off the accursed "investigation" into Brad's death, which she was now more than ready to give up as purposeless, unkind, and a general waste of mental effort. On the other hand, she had not yet breached the real mystery of the missing Civil War soldiers. Perhaps a new puzzle would clear the other, more recent events out of her mind.

Despite much opposition from old-time residents, the library had recently been moved from its original picturesque, but increasingly cramped, quarters in a 19th-century brick building on the Green, to a new, less quaint but decidedly less mildewy building just beyond the Music Faire where the state highway picked up again from Elm Street on the east side of town.

Diana had not joined the preservation-at-all-costs brigade on that occasion and was pleased with the roomy, well-lit new library, which housed the Historical Society research collection in a separate wing. When she went to the library in the normal way, it was to find books, to read an out-of-town newspaper, and to sit in a quiet corner and do what she came for, and so she had told Enid Peterson when asked for her signature on a petition to preserve the old library. If she could do all that better in a newer building, with good lighting and up-to-date climate control, then she was all for it. Enid had gone off in a snit, saying she would never have believed it of her.

The old library was now a day-care center, much appreciated by mothers of small children who might otherwise never visit the old town center, and the Green still looked exactly as it always had, a long narrow swath extending three blocks down the center of town, with no intrusive modern buildings or storefronts or neon signs to disturb its beauty. What kinds of businesses went on behind those pristine exteriors was immaterial to Diana.

Leaving her Volvo in the library's spacious parking lot, Diana headed directly to the Historical Society collection, waving a greeting to the librarian on duty as she passed, then sat down in a comfortably padded chair in a corner and pulled out of her book bag a notebook and the information Cynthia Howell had faxed to her after the Society meeting. This consisted of the preliminary report from the professor who had examined the skeleton *in situ*, as well as a list of Middleford men who had served in the Civil War, including the fifteen Diana had designated MIA. One of them, she was convinced, was the skeleton in her yard. She was looking for some connection between any of those men and the inn as it was in the 1860s.

She located the documents she needed easily on the shelves, which were set up in chronological order—much more accessible than they had been in their tightly packed shelves in the old library—and found the Army records of the local regiments before she even sat down to make a detailed study.

She was not entirely sure how she would identify the skeleton from her yard as one of the missing men, except by the same methods she and Jane and Beth had been using in their investigation of Bradford Gray's death, so she laid the list of the fifteen missing men in front of her and began comparing the names to those in the Army records, to eliminate those whose final days were officially accounted for. She'd show that Loretta Chase about historical research.

Dismissing this unworthy thought, she went through her lists methodically and soon eliminated six names, men who had died in Army hospitals in another state, one who had been court-martialed and imprisoned in Washington, D.C.—wouldn't Loretta love that bit of information—and two who had moved to different parts of the state without coming home to Middleford first.

Diana paused at the second account, wondering why those men didn't come home. Had they been without families, without roots in the community, perhaps without property after so long an absence? Perhaps there was a Bradford Gray a hundred and fifty years ago who discouraged them from coming home. Why would that have been?

She shook her head. This was her imagination spinning nonsense, and unprovable nonsense at that. She went back to the black-and-white facts and found another man who had lost a leg and ended up fading away in a convalescent hospital—not the one that had been set up briefly in the inn, fortunately—and dying even before Appomattox.

She made a note to call the professor and ask if the skeleton showed any distinguishing marks, such as a missing leg or another kind of wound. She supposed that a bullet that hit a bone, even if not fatal, would leave a mark.

She had forgotten how much she enjoyed this kind of research, which she had rarely done since college, except to search the town's official property records for ammunition against Brad Gray and his opposition to her opening the inn. She had no trouble locating personal information about most of the Civil War veterans as well as their official records, and it made fascinating reading. She found she could locate some of the soldiers' homes by the addresses on the letters, and thought she would visit those houses, if they still existed, sometime soon.

The majority of the Historical Society's information, of course, was about Captain Gurden Gray, the local hero. She only glanced at this, convinced that everything that could be unearthed—so to speak— about Captain Gray had already been done by his proud descendants. She concentrated on the lesser-known names, names she could not remember hearing before, but which came to life in her active imagination as she read.

"Are you all right in here, Diana?" Irene Fairholm's voice, with its trained librarian's quiet clarity, penetrated her abstraction.

"Hello, Irene. I'm fine, thanks."

"It's just that you've been in here for hours and—"

Hours? Diana glanced at her watch. Good heavens, it was almost six! She'd said she would be home for dinner, having invited Margo to join her. Margo would be wondering what had happened to her. As if on cue, her stomach rumbled.

Irene laughed. "I thought you might have forgotten to eat."

Red-faced, Diana started pulling her things together, saying, "I guess I'd better get home."

"You can leave those books out if you're coming back. Not too many people use this room, and if someone does come in, I'll put them aside for you."

"Thanks. Oh, by the way, Irene—you don't happen to know where in town the other Civil War veterans are buried, do you?" It had just occurred to her that she might eliminate more names on her list by finding the graves of the missing men. In theory, at least, that would prove they had not been buried in her yard, although, of course, if they had not been interred in Middleford, or the monuments were only that and did not mark an actual grave, she'd be back where she began.

"I suppose most of them are in the old burying ground," the librarian said, "but there's also the Hickory Hill cemetery. That goes back more than a century. And there are a couple of old family plots out along Route 31—I know of one behind the farm market."

"Oh, yes, I know where you mean. Thanks, Irene."

She left, none the wiser about the identity of her skeleton, but grateful to have been able to get away from present-day deaths.

Chapter 24

By the weekend, the excitement had died down, thanks to Kent's assurances that while the death of Jackson Miller was a tragedy, the circumstances indicated that no one who lived in Middleford had anything to do with it. No further mention was made of a serial killer, so while the "case" was still talked of, almost everyone went back to their usual business. Which on this weekend meant the opening of the Festival for the season.

Even Beth had reorganized her priorities and called to say she'd snagged an interview not only with the young leads in *Romeo and Juliet*, but with the visiting star himself, Alex Gordon. She would not, she said, be able to come to another meeting with Diana and Jane if she were going to get this into the next edition of the *Weekly Citizen* along with a review of the opening. Cynthia Howell had taken on this unenviable task, which Beth distributed among her various friends and employees each year so that no one critic risked incurring the wrath of the theater population more than once.

"Have you ever given them a bad opening review?" Diana asked.

"Well, no, but we try to be fair, particularly since they don't pay us to do their publicity. I'm hoping that if this production is less than optimal, my interviews with the leads will make up for it. Next year I may start the season with a special festival edition—no reviews—

so that if necessary, I can pan them the following week and hope they don't notice."

"From what I've seen of this production, Cynthia can write a glowing review with a clear conscience," Diana assured her.

She then called Jane, who offered to drive them both to the theater after announcing gleefully that she'd received a complimentary ticket that very morning from Alex Gordon, so naturally she was planning to attend.

"That's a first," Diana said, not revealing that Jane's ticket came from a block of them Alex had given her to distribute as she saw fit. "I thought you preferred to wait for a matinee when you can concentrate on the play, not the audience."

"I'm open to new experiences," Jane said, "particularly when I don't have to pay for the ticket myself."

Diana laughed and agreed to let Jane drive her to the theater, reasoning that there was always someone willing to drive her home again.

By late afternoon, Diana found herself caught up in the excitement too. There was an air of expectation mixed with panic hanging about the house, as the actors raced around looking for clothing they were already wearing, or reading lines to each other, or trying to sleep with nightshades over their eyes and pillows over their ears. Diana kept them supplied with coffee (to the line readers) and aspirin (to the nappers). It was its own kind of performance, she thought with a fond smile, observing from her kitchen.

By seven o'clock, she was ready and surveying herself in her mirror. She'd elected not to be inconspicuous and wore a scarlet, spaghetti-strapped dress, simple but revealing too. Too revealing? she wondered, smoothing the silk over her tummy. It stayed flat when she removed her hands. It would do.

The first night of the Festival season, traditionally scheduled for the first Sunday in June, was always a glittering affair, but because this was also the opening night of the twenty-fifth anniversary of the festival's founding, the organizers went all out. As the widow of the founder, Diana had an automatic entrée and the best seats in the house. This time she gave the second seat to her housekeeper, since she hadn't had a chance to offer it to anyone else, and in any case, she preferred to have a friend sitting beside her tonight.

Jane let her off at the entrance before she went off to find a place to park. Diana was to meet Margo in front of the theater half an hour before curtain, but when she got to the door, Margo hadn't, or she was lost in the crowd.

"More than likely just couldn't find a place to park," Kent Brewster said when Diana approached him. Kent was on duty tonight, as on every opening night, stationed at the entrance and patrolling the Terrace Café next door on the lookout for drunk-and-disorderlies.

"I think she was planning to walk," Diana said, watching theater patrons drift in, aglow with excitement, the warm night, and the only chance they had all year to dress up. "Or at least park near Town Hall and walk the rest of the way."

Kent had his hat pulled down to hide his eyes, a habit of his that Diana found disconcerting because she could not look directly at him. She assumed he did it so he could observe the comings and goings without being seen to do so, but it still made her feel a little awkward. Nonetheless, she had approached him deliberately.

"Thanks, Kent, for being kind about Jackson Miller. I hear you got the funeral parlor to give him a grave marker."

His stiff stance eased a little. "Well, we haven't located any family yet, and his remains were ... um, long past being ready to bury. Besides, he was part of the town in his own peculiar way."

"He was that," she said. "I for one will remember him."

When he made no further comment, she said, "Is Larraine here tonight, Kent?"

"No, she wasn't feeling real well, and you know she hates crowds."

"I did notice at the Historical Society meeting that she was a little ... pale. Is there something specific wrong with her?"

He did look at her then, tilting his hat back. "Why?"

She shrugged. "I just wondered. I'll go see her tomorrow if you think—"

"I don't. Stay out of it, Diana."

"What do you mean?"

"I know you've been snooping around, asking people if they saw Brad the day he died, badgering Mrs. Mallory for information—"

"I did not badger her!" Diana exclaimed, indignant.

"—Sending Beth Hudson to dig up the autopsy report. Just what do you expect to find, Diana?"

"I didn't expect anything. Oh, look, Kent, please don't think I'm trying to do your job. It was simple curiosity, that's all."

He grunted, which she took to be a sign of disbelief. She tried a different tack, even while her better self told her to drop it.

"But suppose Brad didn't die accidentally, Kent? The autopsy said 'probable accident,' didn't it?"

"Why isn't 'probable' good enough for you?"

"I guess it is, if you say so. But don't you want to know for sure?"

When he didn't respond, she joked, "You won't have to retire on an unsolved case if I solve it for you, will you? I'll give you all the credit—I promise."

"Diana," he said, slowly, as if to a dull child, "there is no case."

Just then, Charlie Pettibone came up to his boss and said there was a fight going on in the parking lot. Kent headed off in that direction, but not before he said to her in an enough-is-enough tone:

"Stay out of it, Diana. I'll take care of it."

"What was that all about?" Jane said, having located Diana by looking out for her red dress. It hadn't occurred to Diana to ask Jane what she was wearing, but Jane was, as always, the practical one, in a blue sheath and pearls, with flat shoes and a purse only large enough to stow her program.

"I'm not sure," she said. *Take care of what?* she wondered.

Lights began to flash, and audience members still outside the theater began to surge inside. Margo found her, also by looking for her dress, and they rode the wave into the auditorium, finding their seats only minutes before the curtain went up. Jane leaned over from her own seat in the row behind her but had time to say only, "Let's talk at intermission," before the theater darkened.

Once again, Diana found herself caught up in the magic of theater, again astounded at the change in the people she saw every day when they became someone else for the course of the play. Alex's entrance caused a murmur and refocusing of attention on the stage, which at this early point in the play still hung half in and half out of the auditorium. Alex brought them all into his orbit.

It was a fast-paced production, full of youthful energy and emotion. Juliet was a pale, sweet-faced girl who really looked fourteen, and Romeo was a force of nature, ready to take this delicate creature to heights of passion with a touch so gentle that it seemed foreign to him, yet entirely natural.

Diana was so caught up in the magic that it was several minutes after the act curtain came down before she came back to reality.

"Liked it, did you?" Jane said, smiling, as they headed for the members' lobby and a respite from the crowd—as well as free drinks and a buffet.

"Didn't you?" Diana asked, astonished that anyone would not.

"Very much. I just come back to earth faster than you. Let's have a canapé." Jane made a beeline to the buffet table and had no shame about loading up a plate "for both of us."

Diana laughed and added a sliver of toast and pâté to the pile.

"I knew I wouldn't have to eat dinner," Jane observed. "They always have such wonderful food on opening nights. Get me a glass of wine from that waiter, would you?"

Diana obliged, taking one for herself as well. "I think you like that eggplant *à la Greque* better than Shakespeare."

"Better than oatmeal cookies. Almost better than Cherry Garcia."

"There's the post-show party as well, you know. You're still invited. Save some room for that."

Jane shook her head. "Not me. Even short Shakespeare is an hour too much. I'm for my bed as soon as everybody dies.

"You go," she added slyly. "I'm sure you'll find someone to keep you company."

Diana stuck out her tongue, but well acquainted with Jane's early-to-bed habits, she did not urge her further.

Taking their full plate of hors d'oeuvres and their wine to a slightly calmer corner, they held their abbreviated meeting. Jane reported nothing new, and Diana recounted part of her conversation with Kent outside the theater.

"Did you have a chance to call Larraine?" she asked.

"Yes, but she was on her way out of the house, so we made a date to get together tomorrow afternoon."

"That's odd," Diana said.

"What?"

"Kent told me she wasn't feeling well. Where would she go out to?"

"Doctor's appointment? She wouldn't have been likely to tell me that, being none of my business."

"Well, all right, I'll concede that. But the other thing is ... we have a date for tomorrow as well. I wonder if she forgot. What time are you supposed to meet?"

"For lunch at the Colonial Café."

"Oh ... well, I suppose that's more than enough time for her to get to my house afterwards. Call me when you leave her, will you?"

"Sure."

The lights dimmed for the second act and, not sorry to leave this subject, both women hurried back to their seats. The rest of the play, indeed, energized Diana so that afterwards she lingered in the lobby, talking to other innkeepers and old friends for some time before saying good night and heading around to the stage door, where Nigel was waiting for her.

"There you are! I'd hoped you hadn't forgotten."

She heaped him with the praises for his performance that she knew he hoped for, and fully deserved, and let him lead her inside, where she was immediately surrounded by actors still high on a performance well played. Diana had seen this phenomenon before, as the actors walked back home after a good night, a foot off the ground, laughing and insulting each other's performances and generally pleased with their world. It was for that reason more than any that she had given them an hour after each performance to wind down before quiet hours went into effect. Anyone who wasn't ready to collapse into bed at that point headed to the Cyn Bin—which was wisely located on a remote side street where the neighbors wouldn't be disturbed by all-night revels.

The cast party after the performance, however, was held at the Festival Inn, which had no real connection to the Festival other than its name—changed a few years ago from the Lakeside Inn—but had the facilities to host a large party. As they walked in, Nigel was kidnapped by several of his fellow actors, leaving Diana on her own. She let him go, not entirely sorry. She still was unsure how to treat him anymore, which was an uncomfortable feeling since they'd been easy friends for so long.

She turned, looking for Alex—and instead found herself face-to-face with Marjorie Gray, on Mark Edwards's arm.

"Hello, Diana," she said, giving Diana another few seconds to recover from her shock as she turned to her escort. "Mark, dear, will you give us a moment?"

"Of course." Mark backed gracefully away, but not before winking at Diana, which she was not sure how to interpret but suspected he was telling her not to make too much of Marjorie's possessiveness. Good heavens, Jane *would* be sorry to have missed this party after all.

"How are you, Marjorie?" she said, infusing as much warmth into her voice as possible to make up for her uncharitable thoughts. To her consternation, Marjorie's eyes welled with tears, but she caught them before they spilled over, almost as if she could will her body's natural functions to do her bidding. Perhaps she could.

"I just wanted to thank you, Diana—for the flowers, I mean."

"There's no need," Diana began, uncomfortable again. She had sent flowers in lieu of a condolence call, which she had not felt up to making, considering her prurient interest in Marjorie's husband's death.

Marjorie put her hand on Diana's arm. The multi-diamonded ring on her slim fourth finger glittered in the artificial light. "There is. You're the only one who thought of me, Diana, and I want you to know I'm grateful. Everyone else sent flowers to the funeral, or in Brad's name, but your card was addressed just to me. I know we haven't been the best of friends, but that was very thoughtful."

Diana managed a smile. "I'm glad I could help, Marjorie. It was the only thing I could think of."

Marjorie removed her hand and for a moment did not seem to know what to do with it, there not being a man's arm close by to take hold of. She placed it beside her other hand, clutching a gray silk purse that perfectly matched the discreet mid-calf length, long-sleeved gray silk dress she wore.

"Well ... I'll leave you to enjoy the party, Diana."

With that, she slipped away before Diana could think of anything else to say. She stood for a moment reflecting on the odd things that a death in the family could reveal about a person. No doubt next week Marjorie would be back to her old, self-absorbed habits and forget that for a moment she had been grateful for the kindness of a relative stranger, but her uncharacteristic—yet true—gesture tonight had warmed Diana's heart with sympathy for a complicated but not so unnatural woman.

She sighed, then looked around again for Alex. Not seeing him, she began instead calculating whether she had room at the inn to host a party of this size next season. She didn't have any large rooms, but all the ground-floor rooms connected, so she supposed she could use the whole floor, uniting the rooms with a similar decorative motif. Perhaps, since opening nights were all in flower season, masses of them in every room … or better, a theme based on the play being opened....

"What are you thinking?" Alex said, approaching her just then.

She smiled. "I was beginning to think like Martha Stewart."

"Good grief. Let me know if you're in danger of doing that again, and I'll be sure to stop you."

He was looking very elegant, she couldn't help noticing, in an actual tuxedo. Auditioning for the part of artistic director, perhaps? She was about to tease him about it when Romeo and Juliet made a belated entrance and received the ovation that first-night stars of any magnitude were due. They both seemed delighted at the reception, Romeo trying to look cool, but Juliet hugging everyone in sight and giggling with her friends over spritzers.

Alex asked Diana what she cared to drink, and sat her down at a table. By the time he returned, however, she was surrounded by the same crowd she'd attracted backstage, who after cheerful greetings, were soon ignoring her to lobby verbal bricks at each other. Alex signaled her to come with him, and she got up to join him.

"Do you want this?" he said, and when she shook her head, he handed her drink to Tybalt, who had just arrived looking miffed that no one noticed his entrance. He took the glass, then seemed to realize who had given it to him, and said, not very graciously, "Thanks."

They met Mark Edwards—alone—outside. "Aren't you staying?" he said.

Alex shook his head. "The night's for the two youngsters. Go and make them feel like stars. And don't mention any notes tonight."

Mark grinned. "Practicing for the job already, are you?" Then he remembered Diana and looked toward her questioningly.

"It's all right," Alex said. "I've told her."

"I see." Mark smiled at Diana, then turned it exaggeratedly on Alex. "I guess I'll see you when I see you. No need to come to the run-through tomorrow."

"I'll be there," Alex said.

Not sure what undertones she wasn't reading into that exchange, Diana followed Alex to the street. "Did you drive here?" he asked.

"Jane drove me, but she's gone home."

"I'll take you back, then."

They were silent on the short ride, but the silence inside the car was different somehow, as if the tensions of their last meeting had somehow dissipated. Diana was not sure of the reason for this, but she was glad ... and apprehensive. What did it mean? Was she prepared for whatever happened next? Why did she always wait to see what happened instead of initiating it herself?

The house was so quiet when they arrived, in comparison to the noisy party, that it seemed to be in a different world. They stood together in the parking lot for a minute until Diana said, "Will you come in for a drink or something?"

He smiled and stepped closer to her. "I was thinking of 'something,' but not in your house." He put his hands on her bare arms and ran them lightly up and down; she shivered at the incredibly erotic touch and felt her skin become sensitized all over her body. "Am I still welcome at the gatehouse?"

She smiled. "It's still yours. I haven't changed anything."

They walked around the house to the smaller building. Alex glanced toward the site where the skeleton had been found; the earth had been raked over and tamped down, but it was still black against the green surrounding it. He made no comment, but kept his hand on hers, and she could think of only that.

Inside the gatehouse, he closed the door without turning the light on. Pale moonlight drifted in the windows, and she examined his features minutely in it as he gazed at her, then leaned over to kiss her.

"I didn't tell you exactly what it was I did want from you," he said, when he released her mouth, leaving her breathless. "Do you know?"

"I do now," she said. "I want it too. I knew that when you first came here, I think. I just haven't been able to acknowledge it to myself."

"It takes courage, giving yourself to someone else. You could be hurt."

"I don't think so," she said, and reached her hand up to bring his head down.

"Make love to me, Alex," she whispered, kissing him.

He slid the straps of her dress down her shoulders as he deepened the kiss, then found the side zipper and pulled it slowly down, letting the dress fall to the floor. She reached out for him and began removing his jacket, then his shirt, until she found the warm skin, sensitized to her own, underneath.

He took her to the bedroom.

Chapter 25

Diana had become accustomed to waking up alone in the years since Daniel died, and had come to value her time alone, her privacy. So why did she feel acutely lonely this morning? She glanced over to the other side of the bed. Not only had Alex gone without waking her, he'd scarcely left a mark. The sheets were smoothed, the pillow plumped, the door closed. She supposed that he was being careful in case someone came in unexpectedly—although anyone who did would certainly wonder at her spending the night in the gatehouse. It was thoughtful of Alex just the same. But she wished the room didn't seem as if he'd never been there, never made sweet love to her in the quiet of the night.

She sighed. In a minute, she'd be positively maudlin. It had been wonderful, a night to remember. Alex had been a tender, thoughtful lover. Why couldn't she remember only that? Why did she look for something to blame herself for?

She jumped out of bed, glanced out the window, and wondered if she could get to her own room without being seen. It was still early. The actors would certainly not be up, even if they were home, and Margo wasn't scheduled to come in until eleven. She decided to brazen it out, pulled her discarded dress back on, and let herself out. She crossed the lawn in full view of the house, daring any unknown onlookers to wonder where she'd been, and slipped in by the kitchen door.

She showered and hurriedly changed her clothes, then went downstairs. She'd throw herself into work. After all, the inn could open this summer, next month if they had enough rooms ready. And Vitelli had finally finished in the yard. She snatched up the telephone as she passed the extension in the hall and dialed the plumber's number, getting Mrs. Vitelli, who informed her that Romeo wasn't at home. Hadn't Mrs. Quick seen him? He'd said he'd get the lawn seeded today. Oh, and thank you so much for the tickets to the show.

"We had a wonderful time," Maria gushed. "So many people, such excitement. We saw Donald Sutherland and got his autograph! I was so thrilled."

Diana tried to tell her that Mr. Gordon had provided the tickets, and she should thank him—no doubt he was accustomed to handling adoring fans—but Maria was still talking. No wonder, Diana thought uncharitably, that Romeo had wanted to get out of the house.

But she listened because, oddly enough, Maria's artless enthusiasm reignited her own pleasure in the evening ... and its aftermath. She agreed that it was a wonderful production, that the leads were just charming, the sets and costumes amazingly like Italy.

"Thank *you*, Mrs. Vitelli," Diana said for the sixth time, and finally hung up the phone. She smiled and made a mental note to provide tickets for the Vitellis again next opening.

"What was that all about?" said Margo, who'd been leaning against the door jamb with a dust cloth in her hand for several minutes.

Diana laughed. "Don't ask. Is it true that Vitelli is almost finished?"

"It's true. Look for yourself. If he does the seeding today, you should have nice grass in a couple of weeks, what with the warm weather settling in. But before you go out, come up to the first floor landing and tell me which pictures you'd rather have hanging there."

Diana spent the morning seeing to last-minute details in the bedrooms at the Green side of the inn, the ones with the best view and the ensuite bathrooms, which would book up fast, Jane had assured her. They were also far enough distant from the common areas of the inn that she wouldn't have to ask the actors to move out just yet. Although the gatehouse was technically empty now.

She wondered suddenly why Alex hadn't invited her to his rented home last night. Perhaps it was just that he wanted her to be able to be at home when she needed to be. Perhaps it wasn't a very inviting house ... not that she would have cared last night. Enid had said it was in one of the newer developments, which generally meant lots of amenities but not much charm. She shrugged and told herself it didn't matter, but this self-reassurance had barely crossed her mind when she began visualizing her personal quarters at the Inn on the Green and wondering if they were roomy enough for two....

Between them, she and Margo added the last touches, checked that everything from telephone extensions to faucets to bedside alarm clocks worked as they should, then put fresh linen on the beds and, at last, declared themselves finished.

"Of course, if you don't get a booking for a month, we'll have to change the beds again anyway," Margo pointed out.

"I don't care. It looks ready, it is ready, and I can show it off to the Accommodation Bureau if no one else."

"Time to get listed?"

"Time to declare this ship well and truly launched."

They hugged and jumped around the room like schoolgirls for a moment, until Margo said, "Look out! You'll knock over a lamp."

Diana laughed. "We've got more. There's an attic full of spare parts, remember. I'm going to the Bureau to crow over Enid Peterson." And ask her where exactly Alex was living, while she was about it. "Why don't you quit for the day? There'll be more than enough to start on tomorrow with the two bedrooms on the other side of the landing."

Margo took her up on the offer, and they ended up leaving the inn together, parting company in the parking lot, where Margo got into her Jeep and Diana into her Volvo.

The Accommodation Bureau was an extension of the Mainstage box office, but had its own quarters in the bookshop attached to the outside of the building. Diana went in, told Enid that The Inn on the Green was ready to begin receiving guests, signed the paperwork, and left a supply of the brochures she'd had made up months ago in fond anticipation of an imminent opening, only slightly delayed by Brad Gray's obstructionist tactics at the most recent zoning commission meetings.

Damn. For a few hours, she'd forgotten Brad Gray. To push him out of her mind again, she asked Enid point-blank for Alex Gordon's new address.

"Oh, now, Diana," Enid said coyly, brushing an imaginary bit of lint from her Peter Pan collar, "you know I'm not allowed to give out that kind of information about festival members. We're very careful about their privacy, you know."

Diana leaned on the counter, pretending to be Jane, who did not suffer fools gladly. "Enid, don't be ridiculous. Give me that address or I'll take back my listing. I don't need this office to get paying guests, nor do I need to pay your percentage. I'll remind you that I have the ear of the festival's board and can report any lack of service I see in this bureau to someone who can fire you."

She was beginning to sound like Seth Howell in his best form at a zoning meeting. "Now fork it over."

Enid was more easily intimidated than Diana realized—or she had floored her with her uncharacteristic display of ferocity. Without another word, Enid wrote the address on a piece of paper and handed it to Diana, who snatched it away and, remembering Nigel's advice to get off while you still held your audience, turned to leave without another word.

She got only as far as the door. Behind her, a sob escaped Enid and, astonished, Diana turned around and hurried back to the other woman's side. Enid had put her head down on her desk and was weeping loudly, disregarding the tourist brochures and neat pile of pink telephone message slips that she was spilling tears on.

"Oh, Enid, I'm so sorry," Diana said, appalled. What had she done? She hadn't expected her firm stance to unhinge Enid like this. "I didn't meant to be rude—please don't cry."

Enid pulled several tissues out of a box on the shelf behind her with one hand, and with the other waved dismissively at Diana, who pulled up a nearby chair anyway and put her arm around Enid's thin shoulders.

"It's not that," Enid said after a hearty blow into the tissues, which she dropped into a wastebasket. Diana pulled several more out of the box and handed them to her. "It's nothing to do with you. It's just…"

"Tell me, dear," Diana said, as soothingly as she could.

Enid sniffed. "I'm at my wit's end, is what it is. It's my boy, Howard—my nephew, I mean. Do you know him, Diana?"

Lying only a little, Diana said, "Of course I do. Isn't he staying with you for the—um, for a visit?"

That set Enid's tears loose again, but when she'd calmed down, she said, "He was. He's run away!"

Run away? Diana wondered. Surely Howard wasn't a child anymore, and his parents lived in Springfield, she recalled. Like any self-centered teenager, he probably just never thought to tell his doting aunt that he was leaving.

Enid shook her head. "I called my sister—Howard's mother. He hasn't come home either. She's worried sick. It's all my fault," she finished in a pathetically weak voice.

"It's no such thing," Diana tried to assure her. "Have you talked to Kent about this? I'm sure there's something the police can do—"

"No!" Enid insisted. "I can't tell anyone. And don't you tell either, Diana Quick!" she added, getting some of her former strength of mind back. "Anyway, I'd have given him the money if he'd just asked."

Diana had removed her arm from Enid's shoulder and tried to get up to leave, but this stopped her. "What money?"

Enid hesitated, but Diana stayed put. "I had some cash hidden away at home—for emergencies, you know—and after Howard left, I couldn't find it."

Diana remembered something that Kent said at the press conference about Jackson Miller. She also remembered that Enid hadn't been there. "Was it by any chance in fifty-dollar bills?" she asked.

"Yes, why?"

Diana kicked herself, but she had to know. Improvising on the spot, she said, "The waitress at the

Colonial Café told me someone had left her a fifty-dollar bill for a five-dollar sandwich."

Enid looked relieved. "Oh, that must have been Howard. I wondered where he was getting his meals, since he hardly ever ate at home—at least, not since the first week he was here. But you won't tell anyone he took the money, will you, Diana?"

"Whatever you like, Enid. But please promise you'll call me if you change your mind, or I can do anything to help, or you just want to talk again."

Enid sniffed into the last of the tissues.

"Enid?" she prodded.

"All right. I promise."

"Good girl." She had to leave it at that.

Diana stood outside for a moment and tried to think about something other than Enid's unexpected breakdown and the dilemma she'd put herself into. Of course, she had to tell Kent Brewster about Howard's theft; it didn't mean he killed Jackson Miller, but it was evidence of some connection between them.

She got into her car, but sat there for a moment, trying not to think about the story she'd just heard. Instead she contemplated whether the prices she'd listed in the inn's brochure were too high or too low, whether there was enough food in her pantry to begin serving guests. She gazed at the Festival posters in the window of the Accommodation Bureau and thought about Shakespeare and star-crossed lovers, anything other than murder in her own hometown and annoying petty tyrants who turned out to be as vulnerable as anyone else. She decided to go to the theater to see if Alex was busy.

It had been mere hours since the curtain fell on *Romeo and Juliet*, but Verona had disappeared from the stage. Instead, technicians were measuring and painting and pacing, while downstage, three actors sat in metal folding chairs, scripts in hand, and read their lines in low voices. One of them was Alex.

Diana glanced around and saw Nora Peale and Jim Bishop sitting together in the back of the auditorium, a script on their knees, which they were paying no attention to. Diana hesitated to interrupt, but she saw no one else she knew, so she moved slowly into the row, giving them the option of pretending not to see her. But they were apparently well-raised young people.

"Mistress Quickly!" Jim started to rise, and the script fluttered toward the floor, but Nora caught it. Molly raised her head from the floor, thumped her tail at Diana, and went back to her nap. "Please join us."

"Thanks, but only for a moment. Are you in this play?"

"Just a non-speaking part," Jim said. "But neither of us has seen the *Duchess* before, so we're glad to be able to watch the rehearsals."

"Isn't it wonderful that the festival is able to put on plays like this, that aren't mounted very often?" Nora said. "I hope they keep doing it."

"So do I," Diana agreed. "Much as I enjoyed last night's performance, I've seen *Romeo and Juliet* six times if once, and I'd as soon see something different myself."

Nora leaned over. "Speaking of *R-and-J*," she said, "did you hear about Tybalt? He was poisoned!"

"What?"

Jim intervened. "Nora's exaggerating. He drank something last night that didn't agree with him. I hear he's allergic to any kind of alcohol, so he must have got hold of a spiked drink by mistake."

"Is he all right?"

"He's still in bed, under doctor's orders, but apparently he'll be fine."

Diana had a sudden visual memory of Alex handing her untouched drink to Tybalt as they left the party last night. She assumed it was the brandy-and-ginger she'd asked him to fetch her. Perhaps it looked to Tybalt like plain ginger ale.

Perhaps it wasn't alcohol that poisoned Tybalt. The drink was meant for her.... No! No one could have predicted that her drink would end up in Tybalt's hand. She was getting paranoid.

She glanced at the stage. Alex was standing now, reading his lines, absorbed in creating his character. She was amazed again at his concentration, at how he could shut out the rest of the world and let this foreign personality that didn't really exist grow inside him.

Shutting out the rest of the world. That included her. She shouldn't have been surprised. After all, she couldn't expect to be the center of his universe, as he wasn't hers. As she was determined not to let him be. They both had lives, pasts, loves and passions that had existed before they met. But she'd hoped just the same that they could shut out the rest of the world for a little longer than just one night, and be alone in their own.

She got up and left.

It was still early, and a beautiful spring day, almost summerlike. It made Diana feel the passage of time, as the change of seasons invariably did. But today there seemed to be more urgency to it, if a positive urgency. She walked briskly to her car, and was putting the key in the ignition when she remembered something and turned left out of the theater parking lot instead of right toward home. That cemetery Irene Fairholm had mentioned was only a few miles down the road; she'd go there first, then home.

The state route meandered a bit as it headed south, away from the lake and the town toward farmland, following a creek the way the old turnpike once had, curving into wooded areas that were almost fully leafed now—another reminder that spring was rapidly turning into summer. Diana slowed down, dug her cell phone out of her purse, and punched in the code for home. In a minute, Margo answered.

"And where have you disappeared to?" she demanded, knowing who it was by means Diana had never been able to understand. She didn't need Caller ID; Margo always knew who was on the line. "Romeo told me he saw your car heading out of town."

"Sorry. I'm making a quick stop at—um, at the farm market on thirty-one. Do you need anything—oh, my God!"

Margo's frantic "What's the matter?" fell to the floor with the cell phone as Diana swerved to avoid a car coming at her from the other direction, half in her lane. She barely missed it, thanking her lucky stars for a good steering system and anti-lock brakes, as well as the fact that she had been driving slowly. She pulled off to the side of the road to catch her breath.

The other car had never swerved from its path to avoid her, and as Diana looked back in her rearview mirror, she saw it continue straight ahead, paying no heed to the curve in the road, and head directly for a huge tree.

"No!" Diana shrieked, too late.

The car hit the tree with a sickening crash and the crunch of bending metal and breaking glass. An instant later there was dead silence except for the ping of hot metal suddenly cooling.

"Diana! Answer me! Are you all right?" Margo was still on the cell phone.

Diana picked it up. "Call 911! I'm all right, but there's been a horrible accident. Tell them to hurry!"

Chapter 26

An hour later, Diana was sitting sideways in her driver's seat, her feet out the open door, giving a statement to a state trooper as the ambulance pulled away and a tow truck moved in to begin clearing the wreckage.

"So the driver missed you...?"

"No, I missed her," Diana said, still stunned but her mind perfectly clear now. "She was veering into my lane, so I steered right and missed her and parked here. She kept going, almost in a straight line, I thought, and hit the tree.... Do you think her brakes could have failed, or her steering? Why would she do that?"

"We'll find that out when we check over the car," the trooper said. He was a lanky young man, red-headed and freckled, trying not to look affected by what was likely his first highway fatality. "You say you knew the driver?"

She had recognized her the moment she rushed to the car to see if she could help, hoping against hope that whoever was in the car had survived the crash. But the blood that covered Larraine Brewster's face and the awful angle of her head had told Diana that her neck was broken. She'd tried to talk to her anyway and, suppressing her horror, touched her shoulder, shaking it lightly.

"Larraine, dear, it's Diana. Can you hear me?" She picked up her wrist, so as not to touch the blood on her neck, and felt for a pulse. Nothing. Nor was there any sign of breath. Tears began to flow down Diana's cheeks, as if her heart was filled with sorrow even if it hadn't registered with her brain yet.

How would she ever tell Kent?

"Her husband's been called," the trooper said now, as if he'd read her thoughts. "They got him on the police radio. He should be here any minute."

Suddenly Diana couldn't wait to leave. She couldn't face Kent, couldn't summon the words to comfort him. It was beyond her now. She couldn't get Larraine's dead face out of her mind ... so oddly peaceful in expression, despite the blood covering it. As if she'd fallen asleep in bed and died a natural death.

"May I go now, please?"

"Just a few more questions—"

"I'm sorry, I can't. I have to get home. You have my card. Call me there. Come to see me tomorrow. I don't care. Just let me go now!"

She was getting hysterical, she could tell. The trooper stepped back as if she'd physically lashed out at him. "Yes, ma'am—Mrs. Quick. We'll contact you. You take care, now."

The idiotic cliché almost made her laugh, but she didn't have time to try to explain to the boy trooper that she wasn't insane. She had to get home. To safety and normality and ... comfort.

"Is Mr. Gordon here?" she asked Margo half an hour later, having waited as long as she could to ask after Margo had hugged her and cried with her and made her a cup of tea and sat down with her to listen to whatever she wanted to say. It hadn't been very much. Diana no longer felt anything much beyond fatigue.

"I think he's still at the theater, rehearsing *The Duchess of Malfi*." Margo was not immune to the star's charm and had been researching the play so she could use the ticket he'd promised her with the proper appreciation. "Not exactly a cheerful piece of work, is it?" she said, then seemed to think better of even mentioning it. "Why don't you take a nap?" she suggested. "That chamomile will help."

"I suppose," Diana said, taking a last sip. "Was there any mail?"

"Upstairs on your desk. Nothing urgent. It can wait until tomorrow."

Diana went up and closed her bedroom door, but she didn't feel like sleeping, despite her tiredness. She lay down for a moment, then got up again and looked for her jacket. From the pocket, she pulled a small, fragile, very old book.

She hadn't told the trooper about her find. As she had sat with Larraine, wanting to stay with her until help came, she had glanced around the car and seen the book on the back seat. Unable to resist, she'd reached for it, opened it, and begun to read. It was the Civil War diary Larraine had told her about at the Historical Society meeting. She was meant to have it, she had rationalized, slipping it into her pocket.

She sat in a chair and opened it again now.

Darkness had fallen by the time she remembered the mail and picked it up to see if there was anything she should attend to at once. She smiled at one letter, the first request for a booking they'd received; Margo had marked it with a red star. Otherwise, there were the usual bills, circulars, a reminder to renew her membership in the Festival from some backstage worker who didn't know she was a lifetime member already. And a note with just her name and no address. She opened it. It said:

Stop meddling or you'll be sorry.

Absurdly, her first thought was, *meddling with what?* Then she realized. There *was* something more to Brad Gray's death than appeared on the surface, and she was getting too close to whatever it was. But in another light, after Larraine's accident, she was already sorry. Too late, mysterious poison pen pal.

Suddenly she had a vision of a car coming at her on a winding country road, a memory of the fleeting sensation, just before she yanked at the steering wheel and swerved out of the way, that it was trying to hit *her*.

Chapter 27

I am not a coward, Diana told herself, as she drove north, away from Middleford, away from threatening letters and mysterious skeletons and unsolved murders that now clearly were threats and mysteries and murder. She couldn't just not think about them, but she didn't know anymore what to do about them.

And she didn't know what to do about Alex, either. Why hadn't he called? He couldn't have been at the theater for twenty-four hours running, especially not after the night they'd spent together. It now seemed so long ago.

Why hadn't *she* called him?

She was almost at the cottage, only a mile or so farther along the narrowing, empty turnoff from the state highway that skirted the eastern shore of Mirror Lake. This must be near where Jackson Miller's body was found, she realized, then turned up the volume on the radio to let Tchaikovsky drown out that thought.

She waited until she arrived at the cottage to use her cell phone to check her messages at home. She was not about to use her phone while driving again, even on a deserted back road. She'd forgotten to get her messages yesterday, or read her e-mail, in the chaos of events and her own emotions. Perhaps Alex had called and couldn't reach her and thought she didn't want to speak to him.

She fast-forwarded through dozens of messages, mostly to do with the inn, and two or three hang-ups. Could that have been Alex? Perhaps he was still concerned about her reputation and didn't want to leave personal messages where someone else might intercept them, so he hung up when she didn't answer. She wished for her Caller ID, then laughed at her own desperation.

She could call him, right now, at the theater. Someone would get him.

She sighed and opened the trunk of the Volvo to extract her overnight bag. Not yet. She needed to calm down. To feel at peace again within herself.

It was certainly peaceful here, with no sound but the lake lapping against the shore, a slight breeze playing through the pale green of the trees surrounding the small log cabin she and Daniel had called their retreat. They had called it a cottage, she remembered, because it was built in the era of the grandiose rustic cabins of New York society millionaires in the Adirondacks, and Daniel did not care to be identified with that kind of excess, so he, perversely perhaps, went in the other direction, naming the place Lakeside Cottage, as if it belonged in the Lake Country of England. At least the lakeside part was accurate.

She dropped her bag on the step and searched for the key, kept behind one of the logs. Not very safe, as Daniel had observed, but there was nothing in the cabin to steal and he didn't want the door destroyed just for mischief. In any case, there was an up-to-date alarm system inside.

Diana went in and deactivated the alarm. The main room was just as she remembered it. She paid someone to clean once a week and air the place out, so it always felt lived-in and inviting. She turned the thermostat up, since she hadn't called ahead to have Jerry, the caretaker, light the fire and plug in the appliances. She walked around doing that, touching the furniture, reconnecting with her memories of the place in a time of her life that now seemed very long ago.

She piled some logs on top of the kindling in the fireplace, lit a fire, then sat down on the sofa and gazed into the tentative flames. Did she want to sell this place to Ben McIlvey? She supposed she should. She could put the money into the inn, add more rooms by gutting some of the third floor. She could renovate the gatehouse and start using that.

She wondered if Alex would like the cabin.

She got up and checked the beds. There was clean linen on them; she needn't remake them. She tossed her bag on one of the double beds and opened it. On top of her underwear and makeup bag was the diary Larraine Brewster had bequeathed her. That was how Diana thought of it now. Larraine's telling her about the diary at the Historical Society meeting was a hint, its presence in her car the day she died a sure sign, in Diana's eyes, that she meant for her to have it. She picked it up and returned to the couch in the front room and turned on the lamp.

Larraine's funeral would be in two days, according to Seth Howell's message on her machine, one of the few she had listened to all the way through. She supposed she'd go back for it, but she needed at least one night away. She couldn't face Kent, not after another death close to him.

Very well, yes, she was a coward.

On the drive up, she'd made up her mind to drop the matter of Brad's death. She'd accept it as an accident, even though she now knew that it clearly was something more, and not meddle any further. Beth could do it if she wanted to; she was an investigative reporter at heart, and she could probably take anonymous threats in stride.

It was a waste of her own life to continue the investigation. Hadn't she had enough to fill her time when she allowed Alex Gordon to seduce her into pursuing it? And to what end? Another death, her own life apparently threatened, a friend lost because she could not help her and only made things worse.

And Alex.

She opened the diary as she walked into the kitchen to make a sandwich. Jerry's wife left bread in the freezer and canned meats in the pantry, and sometimes, like tonight, fresh fruit left over from when they came to clean. She could eat while she read.

But the first entry she set her eyes on made her forget hunger, forget her cozy couch. She sank onto a kitchen chair and leaned her elbows on the table.

There was no name on the diary, only the initials GL on the flyleaf, but each entry was dated. They began in 1862 and ended in 1866, so it was an authentic Civil War document, and some entries referred to battles of that war, as Diana had discovered in her earlier cursory reading. However, while the names of generals of the Union Army and other historical figures were spelled out, as were some local ones—including that of her own ancestor, Sarah Sedley, apparently a confidant of the writer of the diary—the people who were the subject of the entries were identified only by initials. Only a few pages of reading revealed why.

"G sets sail today for B," the diarist wrote on June 2, 1862. "I cannot wish for him to stay, despite his leaving us alone to fend for ourselves. He says he will send money, but how will he do so without revealing his location?"

It took some searching to discover why the mysterious G had to go somewhere he would not be found, but on August 8 of the same year, the diarist, who Diana was now certain was a woman, perhaps the mother or wife of "G," wrote:

"I cannot help thinking of poor KJ, alone in the theater of war, unable to write home. His wife and little ones miss him. I offered money but KJ says the payment was more than sufficient. I give them food from the garden, to offer something. The children thrive but yet pine for their father."

Diana paused. Payment? Then she remembered Beth telling her that some well-do-to Middleford families paid to have poor men go to war in their sons' places. Could G have paid KJ in this way, then left the country—B could be Britain, or Brazil, or even Boston—for the duration? Fascinated, and oblivious now of her surroundings, she skipped ahead in the diary to after the war, eager to learn what happened to KJ. Sure enough, on May 3, 1865, GL wrote:

"G returns today to find himself a hero, little having imagined that KJ would so distinguish himself in battle. G takes the praise for himself. We have not heard from KJ, and G says he will have succumbed to fever and will not return, so why not enjoy the fruits of our investment. He disgusts me. I know not what to do."

Diana wished she knew who GL was; she was beginning to feel a fierce friendship for this unknown, but principled woman.

The last entry, on September 18, 1866, read:

"I write this in haste, for my son and I leave for Maine tonight, to my sister. I cannot stay with G longer. Despite surviving that terrible Southern prison, KJ is dead. I know, but cannot prove, that it is by G's hand. I will leave this diary with Sarah and begin anew in Maine, as with my life. God forgive my husband."

Stunned, Diana sat back in her chair. Then, realizing it was almost dark, and it was a very hard chair, she got up and made the sandwich she had originally come into the kitchen for, and put on the kettle. Then she took the diary back into the other room, put more logs on the fire, and curled up on the couch to think.

Her imagination had no trouble putting the few clues she had found in the diary together into a narrative. Further reading would no doubt fill in the gaps. What was more astounding was that she knew now why Larraine had given the diary to her, and it was not just the mention of Sarah's name.

She put her feet up and her head back, and in a few moments had dozed off, images like old movies still unreeling in her mind, telling the story of an old betrayal, perhaps another murder, in Middleford. "Brother against brother" described not only the War Between the States, she thought. And fell asleep.

She was startled awake by a pounding on the door. She jumped up and went to open it, then hesitated. She had left the door unlocked ... suppose it was whoever had written that note? It was dark in the cabin except for the one light she had left on in the kitchen. Should she open the door?

No, that was crazy. Thieves and murderers did not knock on an unlocked door. She shook her head clear of fantasy and opened the door.

"Alex. Oh ... oh, Alex, I'm so glad to see you!"

She fell into his arms, and he could scarcely close the door and come into the cabin while she clung to him. Then he returned the embrace with passion, and it was several moments before they could tear themselves apart.

"Why didn't you return my calls?" he said.

"You didn't leave a message," she countered. "Where were you all day anyway? I thought you didn't—"

"Didn't what?" he said, knowing the answer.

"Didn't care about what happened last night."

"Can you really think that?"

She smiled and shook her head. "No."

He kissed her again, and a little while later, they went into the bedroom, and for a long while after that, the world returned to the lovely place it had been not so long before. Even later, Diana sighed and stretched, then turned to him.

"Are you awake?"

"Just thinking."

"Tell me."

"I remember now," he said. "Redheaded teenager, jeans and a Mills College T-shirt miles too big for her, granny glasses, beautiful eyes. I had to imagine those eyes behind the glasses, of course, because she rarely looked up, but when I remembered her doing it, I knew they were your eyes."

It was a moment before she realized what he was talking about. She smiled. "The first time we met, yes. I always dressed like that then. I'd forgotten it myself—and I'm amazed, not to mention a little appalled, that you remember."

"I have a good memory. It just goes on leave occasionally."

She laughed. "I'm not sure that's not a good thing. Do you remember the second time, too, or was Daniel all you saw then?"

"I was back ten years later, after D.C. Dickson and all that hoopla. You were married to Daniel then?"

She told him how it had come about, how she had fallen in love with Daniel's strength, and only recently realized how much she had used it as a crutch. Amazingly, he seemed to understand.

Alex...."

"Hmmm?" He was kissing her throat, which made it hard to think.

"What's happening at home?"

He sighed and sat back. "There's news," he admitted but stopped as if censoring what he would say until she punched him in the arm.

"What?"

"Well, first I should assure you that our Tybalt is back on his feet—it was indeed alcohol poisoning, and after the doctor was convinced he wasn't an alcoholic— I'm sure he thinks all actors must be—just very sensitive, he prescribed the right cure."

"That's good news," she said. And her paranoia was beginning to look just as curable. There was undoubtedly an equally simple explanation for Larraine's car accident and the letter warning her to ... but she wouldn't tell Alex about that until she found the explanation herself.

"There's some semi-good news about the body in the woods too," he said. "They found out who did it."

This made her literally sit up and take notice. "Oh, my God—who?" She had kept her promise to Enid Patterson, at least thus far, so how would anyone have found out about Howard's movements, much less put a motive to them?

"I heard this from Beth Hudson, whom I called when I couldn't reach you. She, by the way, thought I should tell you all this immediately, so you'd come back and be yourself again. I didn't ask what she meant by that.

"Anyway, our local constabulary apparently had a visit from a big city cop—one Ray Cooper of the

Albany Police Department. He must have fancied a drive in the country, so he came in person to break the news to Mrs. Peterson."

"Enid? So it *was* Howard?"

He frowned at her, but she didn't explain. "None other. The city police found him dead of an overdose and tracked his movements back here to Middleford, goodness knows how, so Cooper came to compare notes with Chief Brewster.

"Ms. Hudson couldn't have been more excited about a story," he added. "I hope it doesn't knock our poor theatricals off the front page."

"Only for a week," Diana assured him. "News is always a seven-day wonder here, until Beth decides to go to a daily schedule, but that will never happen."

They were silent for a while, Diana thinking over his news, and only vaguely aware of Alex's admiring gaze on her face, as if he were looking for clues to her thinking.

"We have to go home," she said finally.

"Good. Now?"

She laughed. "I suppose it can wait until morning."

"What's the hurry?"

She didn't want to break the mood, but she knew it was very important.

"We have to talk to Kent Brewster."

She told him why.

Chapter 28

"You really didn't have to do this," Diana said again as she raised the knocker on the Brewsters' door. Over the years Kent and Larraine had converted their old farmhouse into a home that was both livable and a landmark in a town where tradition tended to be preserved in aspic and put on display, not lived in and made to fend for itself against the dirt and distractions that life brought in the door. Diana had tried to keep 18 Pennyfeather Lane in her mind as she converted her inn back to its own former life.

"No problem," Alex replied blandly. She didn't argue with him. Despite her much soothed nerves, she was still apprehensive about what sort of reception Kent would give them.

There was no answer to her knock. She tried again, more loudly.

Alex glanced into the window nearest the door. "I don't see anything. Is there a backyard?"

They had called the police station before coming, and according to Charlie Pettibone, the Chief was off duty today and had told them to call him at home in case of emergency. Diana felt a stab of fear. Kent had always seemed so level-headed, but under strain, was he likely to do something desperate?

"There's a patio in the back," she remembered. "We can go around the garage."

They took the graveled path around the side of the garage, which Alex stopped to investigate. "The cruiser's in there. I guess he isn't expecting to go anywhere in a hurry, if he closed the garage door."

Diana hesitated. "You don't suppose...."

Alex put his nose to a crack and sniffed. "No smell of gas. Anyway, there are so many cracks and knotholes in this garage that trying to asphyxiate yourself in it would be an exercise in frustration."

Diana winced, but knew he was right. They continued around the garage and came to the back of the house. Kent wasn't there either, and there was no sound from inside the house.

"Wait here," Alex said. "I'll just walk out to the barn and look around."

"All right." Diana was convinced that Kent must have gone on some mundane errand and would be back any second. Or perhaps he had gone to the cemetery. She remembered, after Daniel's death, wandering around scarcely aware of where she was, although people she met told her later that she'd seemed much like her normal self and spoke to them naturally. Diana didn't remember any of it.

Unlike the inside of the house, which Diana knew Larraine kept as neat as any showplace, the patio was cluttered, mainly with Larraine's potting projects, none of which, on closer inspection, seemed to have been worked on for some time.

On a jumble of tables and benches near the gate to the storage barn Alex had gone to explore, Larraine's restoration project from the old burying ground seemed to have drawn her attention more recently than anything else. Two or three marble slabs, cleaned and the letters restored, leaned against the brick wall. On one table, a jumble of marble pieces, some new and others stained and crumbling, lay about in no discernible order. Diana picked one up.

"What are you doing?"

The voice startled her, and she dropped the piece of tombstone she was holding. "Kent! Good heavens, you gave me a start."

"What are you doing?" he repeated, and there was no mistaking the menace in his tone.

"I—nothing. We—Alex and I—came to ask—I mean, to offer our condolences about Larraine. I'm so sorry, Kent, that I couldn't come to the funeral, but I— well, I just couldn't. And I wanted to tell you about the diary—you know, the one the Historical Society was all excited about, and—"

"What are you doing out *here*?"

"Looking for you, that's all. We knocked—" It was becoming clear that there was something here that Kent didn't want her to see. She glanced around, frantic, wondering what it could be at the same time that she tried to reassure him without upsetting him further that she hadn't seen anything. What could be wrong? What had she done? She'd never seen him like this.

"I—I'd forgotten that Larraine was working on restoring the old marble tombstones in the burying ground," she said, gesturing at the table. "I'm afraid I may have damaged this one...."

She reached down and picked up the piece she'd dropped. It was the jagged corner of an old tombstone, with a brown stain on the broader end.

"Put that down!"

Suddenly, she realized what the brown stain was, and like the last pieces of a difficult puzzle, answers began falling over themselves to fit into their places. She'd discovered the motive in the old diary, and she'd guessed at the opportunity. Here, then, was the means.

"It's the mur—the weapon! I mean—"

Her words caught in her throat when she looked up from the piece of marble at the gun in Kent's hand.

"Put it down, Diana." His voice was coldly calm.

She laid the chunk of marble carefully on the table, not taking her eyes off Kent's gun. Would he really shoot her? Surely not. They weren't alone. Didn't she say she'd come with Alex? What excuse could he make? What would be the point when she didn't know why he was behaving like this?

She was about to ask him, when an implacable voice said, "Put it down, Chief. Walk away from it. That's a good fellow."

Chapter 29

D.C. Dickson to the rescue. Relief flooded through Diana, but she didn't move. There was silence for an endless moment before Kent sighed and let the gun fall to his side.

"Damn it, Diana, why couldn't you leave well enough alone."

He made no protest as Alex quickly came up to him and took the gun away. He removed the clip and put it in his pocket. Then, with one hand firmly on Kent's shoulder, he led him, unresisting, into the living room, where he fell heavily into an easy chair. Alex looked into Diana's eyes and whispered, "Are you all right?"

She nodded, gave him a weak smile, and collapsed onto the sofa. Alex sat down next to her, his side touching hers reassuringly.

They waited for a few moments for Kent to say something, but finally Alex said simply, "Can you tell us about it, Chief?"

The title seemed to register first, and Kent answered, in something closer to his usual voice, "I was due to take early retirement, you know. Only another year. I thought she'd be well enough until then. We were going to go south, sell this place and go where no one would remember…. But she didn't want to leave home."

He stopped and looked toward the kitchen, as if Larraine were still there, happily making supper or washing dishes.

"What was wrong with her, Kent, dear?" Diana asked gently.

His tired eyes focused on her for the first time as a friend. "Early-onset Alzheimer's. It wasn't really noticeable unless you looked hard, and I'd been trying to get her not to go out so much anymore. You know, get her interested in what we'd do when I retired, travel maybe if we didn't sell this place, but you know how she was with that Historical Society and the library and all."

Diana understood then the shifting looks she seen in Larraine's eyes the night of the Historical Society meeting. She must have been drifting in and out of awareness even then, but was still able to control her behavior in public.

"The diary's the key, isn't it?" Alex asked. "Something in it...."

He was trying to lead Kent into a confession, Diana realized. They didn't know anything for sure, even that he knew about the diary, so Kent would have to explain it all, confirm their guesswork all these weeks as well as her conclusions yesterday, which at the time had seemed to make so much sense.

All at once, she didn't want to hear it, didn't want to be put in a position of having to turn Kent in for the murder of his best friend.

But perhaps it wasn't murder. It was still possible that there was some other, simple explanation.

"You don't have to say anything, Kent," she told him, leaning toward him and taking his hand.

He pulled away. "No, I want to. It really was an accident, you know, just not the way I—the way it appeared. That was my fault."

He glanced toward the kitchen again, then spoke hurriedly, as if Larraine would return at any moment. "Brad heard about the diary that day—the day of the zoning meeting—and he came over here demanding that Larraine hand it over to him. She didn't have it, as it happened, having left it at the library, I guess during one of her ... spells. She was going to show it to you, but of course, she ... had her accident first."

"I found it in her car," Diana confessed, reluctant to try to explain her subsequent actions. But Kent didn't seem to find anything unusual about her explanation.

"Oh. Then I suppose she'd already been to the library to retrieve it. Anyway, it made Brad furious that he couldn't lay his hands on it, and I guess at the idea that someone else might read it first and find out family secrets."

"Brad's family?" Diana asked. "But it didn't say anything ..." Puzzled, she tried to remember if any names connected with the Grays or Bonnings were mentioned in the diary, but she could recall only initials. Kent smiled wryly, as if he could guess what she was thinking.

"It was Lorena Gray's diary, Diana. Gurden Gray's sister-in-law, Brad's great-great-something grandmother. She reversed everyone's initials, but once you figured that out—and Larraine did—the story came up clear as day."

"Oh, so GL was LG—Lorena—and so ..." She searched her memory. "KJ was JK, who was somebody Kent, not Kent someone, which puzzled me."

"Judson Kent was my several-times great-uncle. My middle name is Judson; I was named for him." He laughed. "Funny—JK are *my* initials reversed."

Alex was getting impatient. "And what was Judson Kent to Bradford Gray?"

Kent looked at him, seeming to round up his thoughts in a more orderly way, and presented them as if he were addressing a board meeting.

Gurden Gray, according to the diary, paid Judson Kent to go to war in his place—just as Beth had explained, he didn't want to risk the family fortune by dying without an heir—while Gurden sailed to Bermuda and sat out the war under a palm tree. He came back at the end of the war to find himself a hero because Judson, using Gurden's name, had distinguished himself in battle and made a reputation before disappearing in the confusion of Sherman's sack of Atlanta and the March to the Sea.

"Gurden must have thought that a stroke of luck," Alex remarked.

"I guess. The army listed Judson as dead. Unfortunately for Gurden, Judson showed up again, alive, after spending the time in Andersonville prison. I'm guessing Judson was just glad to be home and promised not to say anything. He just wanted to get back to his family."

"But Gurden didn't believe him—about keeping it quiet?" Diana found herself hanging on the story, despite knowing much of it already. But now it was so easy to see Brad and Gurden Gray as cut from the same cloth.

"No, he didn't. Understandably, I guess, considering what he'd done. Anyway, a few weeks later, Judson died, supposedly a delayed result of near-starvation in prison."

"But you don't believe that?" Alex said.

"Lorena didn't. She wrote that Judson's health had been improving steadily until just before he died, when it went downhill fast. She thought to her dying day that Gurden poisoned him."

"Did he?" Diana couldn't help but ask. The diary had stopped before this would have been ascertained.

Kent smiled and shrugged. "What difference does it make now?"

Alex looked intrigued. "If we dug that skeleton up again, and had it analyzed for, say, arsenic poisoning?"

"But what happened that night?" Diana asked again. "When Brad came here looking for the diary?"

Kent scowled. "He scared Larraine, enough that she called me on my cell phone—we have a signal for emergencies that fortunately she remembered and didn't let Brad see. I was close by and came right home. Brad was still foaming at the mouth, but when he saw me, he lit into me instead of Larraine. I could see he was running out of steam, and I was just going to let him rant a while, but then he lunged at me. I ducked, but he was set on a fight, so I decked him. That made him even madder, and he came after me again.

"In that state, he wouldn't have been up to doing much harm, but Larraine didn't know that, and she panicked. She thought he was going to kill me—he looked furious enough, I guess—so she picked up that piece of marble you saw outside and hit him with it.

"It was a lucky blow—if you can call it that. It struck the nerve at the base of the skull and dropped him like a stone. Even I didn't think he was really hurt. I figured he'd been drinking before he came to us and just passed out. I knelt down to check his pulse and realized what happened.

"But I told Larraine she'd just knocked him out. I said I'd take him to the hospital in case he had a concussion. But I knew he was dead. I hauled him out to his car and put him in the trunk. There's probably hairs and fibers and DNA all over it, but I wasn't thinking. I was halfway to the hospital when I decided not to go there after all."

"Why not?" Alex asked bluntly.

Kent shrugged, looking down at his hands, which seemed to find nothing to do with themselves. "Brad Gray always was a bastard, you know. Even when we were kids, he used to bully the little kids—except me. I always stood up to him, and although I wasn't any bigger than he was, I was tough and could lick him in a fight, if it came to that."

"I can't imagine that it ever did," Diana guessed. "Brad wouldn't put himself at a disadvantage."

Kent smiled. "Right you are. He found more devious ways to get to me. He dated Larraine for a while, as soon as he found out I was attracted to her, just to keep me from getting her. But that didn't work either."

So Jane's story was true, Diana realized, even if things hadn't gone exactly the way she'd thought, a simple love triangle. She doubted Brad had ever cared for Larraine, but perhaps she had felt something for him? She remembered all too well that feeling of gratitude a lonely girl has when any kind of attention is paid to her, and Larraine too had been an only child.

"Anyway," Kent went on, "I was damned if I'd let Brad destroy Larraine after he was dead, since he hadn't been able to get to us before. I was going to dump him on his property by the lake, until I realized there was no reason for him to have gone there that night, so I turned around and took him over to the old burying ground instead. I prepared the scene to look like an accident. It *was* an accident, really—it just didn't happen there.

"But I thought I'd have more time. I barely got out of there before you came along, Diana, coming back from the meeting early. Just as well you were dawdling. That's why I went back the next morning, to be sure I hadn't missed anything. As it turned out, I guess I forgot to get rid of that blasted piece of marble in my own house. But damned if you didn't show up at the scene yet again—and you, Gordon. Was that your idea, or hers?"

Neither gave him an answer. Diana said, "You sent that letter, didn't you, Kent, telling me to stop meddling."

Alex gave her a sharp look; she hadn't told him about that and already regretted mentioning it.

"I'm sorry about that," Kent said. "The irony is, I mailed that before Larraine died. If I'd only waited a day, I wouldn't have needed to send it."

He laughed wryly. "I even had an alibi prepared, but you never asked me for one. If you like, you can check the emergency call record for that day and see for yourself. There was a brawl over at D'Agostino's Bar, and I went to break it up. Except I didn't really; that was just a handy way to account for the time frame. I drove Brad's car back to his street and walked back here through the woods ... but you don't care, do you?"

He glared at Alex, but without much heat, as if the fire inside him, which had flared briefly once more, was now thoroughly dampened. He was defeated, and Diana had to feel sorry for him. What would happen to him now? She glanced at Alex, who raised an eyebrow at her, as if to tell her, *You know what to say.*

She said to him, "Will you resign now, Kent?"

He looked at her, his kind brown eyes sad, his voice resigned. "Of course. Everyone knows I've been planning on early retirement—I've been talking it up lately just so. . . Well, you understand. I can say I don't want to stay here without Larraine, which God knows is true enough. People won't question that, unless..." He paused. "Diana, you won't—I mean—" He looked at Alex.

"It's not our business," Alex said. "No one's questioned the autopsy findings, or that Bradford Gray's death was an accident."

No one but everyone she knew, Diana thought, regretfully. Why had she stirred things up with her unthinking mischief-making? Yet how could she have known where it would end?

"What happens now is your choice, Chief. We won't interfere"—Alex smiled apologetically at Diana—"anymore."

"Thank you," Kent said, leaning wearily back in his chair. "I swear, I'll come clean to my superiors, and if they let me, I'll go away quietly. I won't be back."

Diana felt tears well up behind her eyes, but turned her head to quickly wipe them away. Alex rose and took her hand.

"We'll leave you to it, then, Chief."

"Thank you." Kent rose and saw them to the door, as if they'd been paying an ordinary condolence call, and said good-bye on the step.

"Say, Gordon," he called after them. Alex turned around.

"I always liked that D.C. Dickson. Didn't understand what he was saying half the time, but he was a good cop."

"Thanks," Alex said. "Always glad to hear from a fan."

Chapter 30

They drove home in silence until Alex asked, "How about dinner at The Striped Bass?"

Diana smiled. "You liked that place, didn't you?"

"They know what to do with red meat." He glanced at her. "And it's also a nice, private place to talk, without distractions."

"Well, in that case...."

Two hours later, they were again sitting at the window table, savoring their after-dinner drinks, when he asked, "Will Kent keep his word?"

"About resigning?"

"That, and about telling his superiors the truth."

Diana thought this over. "I think he will. They will most likely give him credit for helping to solve Jackson Miller's murder quietly, but he'd want to depart under circumstances that people wouldn't question, and not leave any mystery behind about Larraine. I don't think he cares what comes out about Brad, as long as she's not connected to him in any way."

"You're sure he won't do anything stupid, like...?"

"Suicide? I don't think so. I think Larraine's was too much of a shock."

"You think that's what it was?"

"I'm pretty sure, though I can't prove it. I think she was aware, in her lucid moments, of what was happening to her mind, and she may even have realized, after the fact, that she killed Brad with that marble. So she wanted to end it before she said or did something she couldn't control and got Kent in trouble."

She hesitated, but now was the time to confess everything, so she could forget it all later. "I imagined, briefly and before I knew who the driver was, that the crash was an attempt on *my* life, or at least to run me off the road as a warning. That's why I ran away yesterday. There were just too many frightening things happening, and I didn't know which were real and which figments of my imagination. But I haven't mentioned that to anyone else."

"Nor will I," he assured her.

She looked sadly at him. "Unfortunately, thanks to our meddling, a lot of people have enough information to put two and two together. The question is whether anyone else will announce the result. Fortunately, Mayberry can be discreet when its sympathies are aroused, and everyone likes Kent. They wouldn't want to see him suffer any more than he has."

He smiled. "Mayberry?"

"That's what Jane calls it—affectionately, of course."

"And you, Diana? Will Middleford be enough for you always?"

"Not anymore, no." This did surprise him, while her earlier confession hadn't seemed to affect him. She looked at him, trying to say what she wanted to convey with her eyes, but he waited for her to say the words.

"What else do you want, darling."

"You, Alex. I love you. Will you stay and be part of my world?"

He smiled. "I may never forgive you for making me propose in a restaurant, where I can't make love to you immediately."

"Then we'd better leave now."

Outside, he stopped her before she got into the car. "Diana, there's one thing I should say." He held her gently between himself and car door, as if to be sure she did not escape before he had his say.

She smiled, as if to reassure him that she wouldn't run off again. "Yes?"

"I can't promise to be all things to you, or to include you in my work. I need to retreat into my own self when I'm acting, and you can't come there with me. More important, I want you to have your own world, too, and to love me more because you're happy in that world."

"I understand." And she did.

"On the other hand," he said, as he kissed her quickly, then opened the car door for her, "If I become artistic director, I won't have much time to act."

"And you'll be away from home even more. Thanks for nothing."

He drove home, going once around the Green before turning into the inn's circular drive and slowing a bit. "What do you think?" he asked, rolling down the window.

She looked out and saw it. A brand-new sign that read, in elegant script within a gold frame, "The Inn on the Green."

"Are you responsible for that?"

"Do you like it? It's all kosher with the sign committee, or whoever is in charge of these things here. I called Seth Howell and got him to hurry up the permit, and he did."

"I love it. And I owe Seth a big favor."

He took her hand when she got out of the car in her parking lot, and looked with her at her dream in green and white and soft light coming welcomingly through the windows. And then she looked only at him.

She said, "Welcome home, Alex."

THE END

ABOUT THE AUTHOR

 *Civil Blood* is Elly Kirsten's first cozy mystery, but she's been a fan since reading the classic British cozies of Josephine Tey, Ngaio Marsh, and Dorothy L. Sayers. She grew up in New England, so that seemed a natural choice for a setting for her own mysteries.

As Elisabeth Kidd, she has written ten historical romances, seven of them Regencies. She is the newsletter editor for her local chapter of Sisters in Crime as well as a freelance copyeditor and an instructor for a correspondence school for writers.

www.ingramcontent.com/pod-product-compliance
Lightning Source LLC
Chambersburg PA
CBHW050427260626
47156CB00003B/1186